Horse Stone House

Horse Stone House

By
Harold K. Moon

CFI
Springville, Utah

© 2007 Harold K. Moon

All rights reserved.

No part of this book may be reproduced in any form whatsoever, whether by graphic, visual, electronic, film, microfilm, tape recording, or any other means, without prior written permission of the publisher, except in the case of brief passages embodied in critical reviews and articles.

ISBN 13: 978-1-59955-008-4

Published by CFI, an imprint of Cedar Fort, Inc., 2373 W. 700 S., Springville, UT, 84663
Distributed by Cedar Fort, Inc. www.cedarfort.com

LIBRARY OF CONGRESS CATALOGING-IN-PUBLICATION DATA

Moon, Harold K., 1934-
 Horse Stone House / Harold K. Moon.
   p. cm.
 ISBN 978-1-59955-008-4 (acid-free paper)
  1. Mormon converts--Fiction. 2. Mormon families--Fiction. 3. Immigrants--United States--Fiction. 4. British--United States--Fiction. I. Title.

PS3563.O558H67 2007
813'.54--dc22

2007004793

Cover design by Nicole Williams
Cover design © 2007 by Lyle Mortimer
Edited and typeset by Kimiko M. Hammari

Printed in the United States of America

10 9 8 7 6 5 4 3 2 1

Printed on acid-free paper

One

When it was convenient, Grandmother Winthrop doted on her granddaughters, Catherine and Lydia. And as years advanced, she grew quite generous with some of the jewels she no longer wore, bequeathing a few of the family heirlooms to the girls, thus assuring that the valuables would stay in the family, as was proper and practical. On Catherine's fifth birthday, Grandmother Winthrop brought her an elegant and dazzling necklace, which the girl dutifully allowed her mother to put away for her against the future moment when she would be deemed responsible to wear it properly. To Lydia in the following year, on her fifth birthday, Grandmother bequeathed an emerald bracelet. It was valuable by any standards, and by family standards priceless, and Mrs. Smirthwaite naturally assumed custody of the beautiful piece until her daughter would likewise reach an age of reasonable accountability. But Lydia, knowing where the family jewels were kept, frequently availed herself of what she understood belonged to her, though she could expect periodic lectures concerning her immaturity, which irritated her mightily. Thus, whenever the occasion presented itself, at first through someone's oversight or neglect in locking the velvet-padded safe where family valuables nestled, and later by opening it herself, having surreptitiously learned the safe's combination, she would play with the glittering objects, imagining herself irresistibly beautiful adorned in them from head to toe. She always put on the bracelet first, the bracelet that was to be hers. Her childish wrists were far too small, and the bracelet slid up and down her arm like a hoop on a spindle, but she fancied herself quite elegant indeed. If she heard an approaching step, she would quickly replace the jewels and adopt a pose of indifferent innocence. Occasionally it worked, but not often enough, and each time she was detected she would hear the tedious litany of her character faults, with emphasis on her mischief and immaturity.

<hr />

Squire Smirthwaite cleared his throat. "I noticed a bill posted in the square yesterday. A company of traveling players will perform this afternoon. I thought the girls would enjoy it."

"Traveling players? Those Gypsy people who live on the road?" exclaimed Mrs. Smirthwaite.

"Gypsies? No, I don't think so. Actors. They present shows, and today they'll be in Eccleston. The girls have never seen them, or anything like them. I'm going to give them the pleasure."

"Why would you even consider taking them to mingle with riffraff and ruffians? And you know we must not expose Lydia to places where she might catch something that would affect her lungs. Honestly, Edward, you don't really expect them to glean anything of value from it, do you?"

"Possibly not, but it will do them no harm, either. When I was a lad I enjoyed some jolly entertainment from travelers. They always have shows for children. Puppets and the like. Then they have the usual live show . . ."

"That's the part that worries me, Mr. Smirthwaite, the live entertainment. From what I'm told, it can be rather bawdy."

"I don't remember it being anything but funny. Pure fun, what? Besides, I don't intend to bring any of the players home to dine, nor do I expect to leave my children with them as indentured servants. They're excited to see the show, that's all, and it will be quite innocent, mark my words. As for Lydia—it's summer, and she'll not be exposed to anything threatening."

"And are you taking Myrtle to watch out for them? You can't leave my girls unattended..."

"Of course I can't. But I'll leave Myrtle with you, to attend to her chores as usual. Actually, I thought I might stay with them myself. You wouldn't like to come along, I suppose?"

"Don't be absurd! I do not frequent the public square with wandering minstrels and Gypsies, and I just can't imagine that you would, either. Hardly fitting, is it?"

"I doubt I'll suffer intolerable criticism from my peers for spending an afternoon in the square with my children. Shall I take Judith with us as well?"

"Good heavens, no! She's only three and a half! What would you expect to do with her?"

"Let her watch with us, of course. She can run free a bit if she gets restless."

"Catherine and Lydia are at quite enough risk, I should think. Leave our youngest at home."

***

The morning the girls learned that their father, Squire Smirthwaite, had planned an outing for them, Catherine descended the stairs where Lydia was already waiting. Spotting the emerald bracelet on her wrist, Catherine gasped, "What are you doing? You can't wear that!"

"Why not? It's mine, isn't it?"

"Yes, but you're supposed to wait for it. Mother will..."

"Oh, all right. I can put it back."

She walked into the study where the safe protected their family treasures, pushed the bracelet higher up on her arm, hiding it from view, and returned to Catherine wearing it still, but concealed beneath her sleeve.

***

Squire Smirthwaite stopped his carriage and alighted nimbly before Eccleston Square, lifted eight-year-old Catherine from the back seat, then six-year-old Lydia, setting one girl on his left and the other on his right. He turned to his coachman.

"Come back for us in two and a half hours, Armand. That will give us ample time, I should think."

The coachman nodded and drove away. The girls were already tugging on their father's fingers, eagerly drawing him toward the group gathering around the stall where the traveling players were scheduled to perform. The gaudy curtains hung across the platform that would serve as a stage, and a sizable crowd had already been attracted.

Squire Smirthwaite grimaced. The benches installed temporarily to accommodate the few who were able to pay for the privilege of occupying them were already filled, and the residue, relegated to standing at the rear, were jostling and complaining, vying for the most advantageous view. He spotted a familiar couple some distance away.

"I say, Catherine, isn't that our baker, the one who owns the shop on Wilmot Road where Myrtle usually buys our bread?"

Catherine looked. "Yes. It's Mr. Wengren. Look, Lydia! It's the Wengrens! The whole family. They'll have to stand to watch. Will we have to stand, Father?"

"Possibly not. Come along, let's go see them."

"The Wengrens? Are we going to watch with them?"

"Perhaps. Come along."

The girls followed a bit reluctantly. They had not come to the square to pay a visit to their baker and his family.

"Good afternoon, Mr. Wengren. Mrs. Wengren," the squire said.

The baker nodded happily, smiling broadly.

"Good afternoon, squire, sir," said the missus.

"Mrs. Wengren, would you be so kind as to watch my girls for me? I'll not be long, and it will be worth a shilling if . . ."

"Be most 'appy to watch 'em, squire, but I need no shillin' fer it. Yer can't leave 'em alone, now can yer, and it's no bother fer me ter watch two more."

"But. . ." Lydia began to protest.

"It's only a minute, Lydia. I'm going to see about finding a suitable place to watch the show."

"They'll be fine wi' us, sir. Coom girls."

The squire weaved his way through the crowd, apologizing as he went for the intrusion and then stopped at the edge of the benches, scanning the group seated there, and cleared his throat.

"I should be very grateful if anyone here would accept handsome compensation for making place for three—myself and two little girls."

Silence.

"I would be pleased to make it worth your inconvenience, I assure you."

He heard a grumbling and saw heads wag. "Bloomin' nob, 'e is. Finks 'e can buy us, does 'e?"

The squire straightened, his face scarcely readable, though the knit in his brow might be interpreted as a mildly sour annoyance. He looked about, not expecting his glance to fall on anything specific that might bring fulfillment to his errand but merely attempting to relieve his frustration. Then he recognized that he had been ignoring another need, one he should have attended to before leaving home, and he spotted the area cordoned off and draped with a heavy curtain where gentlemen could relieve themselves, and in his present agitation, the need was suddenly urgent. He strode quickly to the spot, parted the heavy curtain, took care of preliminaries, and set about to help fill the foul-smelling tank that someone would have to empty later. Then he made his way back to where he had left his girls.

On arriving, he found that Mrs. Wengren and Lydia were no longer there; Catherine looked pale and anguished, and Mr. Wengren fared little better.

"Lydia's gone," Catherine said, her lip trembling.

"She were playin' with the girls just there," said the baker. "Then another little girl came and joined them, a girl we didn't know, and then . . . well, I don't know 'ow it 'appened, but my girls came back and Lydia just wasn't with them anymore. Me wife 'as gone to find 'er. I expect she'll be along soon."

The squire scowled darkly and seemed on the verge of a severe remonstrance, but checked himself. He, not his baker, had the responsibility of his children, after all. He glanced quickly about and caught sight of Mrs. Wengren, anxiously inquiring from person to person, gesturing to show Lydia's height and no doubt explaining the child's age, color of hair, eyes, and clothing. It was obvious she was having no success.

"Which are the girls she was playing with?" demanded the squire.

"It were Agnes and Penny," said Mr. Wengren.

"May I speak with them?"

"Of course."

The girls had been standing next to Catherine, sheepish and reluctant.

"What can you tell me, girls? Did Lydia go off with the new child?"

A slow nod.

"You had never seen the other girl before?"

"No, sir."

"Did she just happen to pop in while you were playing, then?"

"Yes, sir. She said she could show us the van."

"The van?"

"Yes, sir. She said the van. She could show us if we wanted to see it. Don't rightly know wot she meant. We came back to ask if we could go. See it, I mean. We di'nt 'ave no permission and we came to . . ."

"Then Lydia went off with her, I suppose. A van, you say?"

"Yes, sir."

"Do you suppose she were talkin' abaht the caravan the show people travel in?" asked Mr. Wengren.

"Don't know. Can't think of anything else it might be. We'd better . . ."

A shriek from Mrs. Wengren cut him short, though she was some distance from them. "Lydia, child! Where did you off to?"

Mrs. Wengren was bustling fast as she could, her legs, foreshortened by excess poundage, churning like a pair of frantic pistons, her ample frame all a-jiggle, her face flushed, toward two little girls who chattered quite amiably as they threaded their unconcerned way through the crowd from somewhere behind the improvised stage.

"Lydia!" shouted the squire.

The two girls stopped, perplexed, as Mrs. Wengren fluttered toward them like a startled partridge from one direction and the squire strode toward them like an invading commandant from another. They stood frozen in place waiting for the two to converge upon them and deliver their sentence.

The sentence turned out to be rather light. Both Mrs. Wengren and the squire were far more relieved than angry, and the girls acquitted themselves adroitly.

"Father, this is Roseanne Withers. She took me to see her house. It's on wheels," Lydia proffered brightly. "Her mother and father are the ones who do the show."

"Ah. Very pleased to meet you, young lady. Lydia . . ."

"We live in a caravan when we do our shows. Mostly we do that in the summer. We don't have a house, but me grandmother has. We stay at her place in winter, sometimes."

The squire noted that the little girl's diction was far better than average and wondered at her origins. He cleared his throat.

"Lydia, you know, I think that you were to remain with Mrs. Wengren while I went to locate seats for us. You had no . . ."

"But . . ." Lydia started.

"But indeed. You ran off while the other girls were asking permission, didn't you? That was terribly rude, Lydia. They were being obedient and you couldn't be bothered."

"I'm sorry, Father."

"Sir, it was my fault," Roseanne volunteered. "Just as the others ran off, I saw me mum leave our caravan to go to speak with Millie—she's another actress in our troupe—and I wanted to show off me mum's costume before she disappeared in Millie's caravan. We had to hurry, so I pulled Lydia with me. She wasn't bein' bad. She was just goin' with me. Please, I hope you won't punish her."

"We weren't gone very long," said Lydia with wheedling contrition.

"Well, no harm done, I suppose. Just remember not to give us such a turn again, what?"

"Did you find seats for us?" Lydia asked.

"All taken, I'm afraid. We may have to stand, but you're up to that, aren't you? Not quite as comfortable, of course, but..."

"Squire Smirthwaite, sir," said Mr. Wengren.

"Yes, Mr. Wengren?"

"We 'ave our place just there. Me daughters 'as found a spot that they feel is comfortable and offers a good view of things. Will you be needin' anything more from us?"

"Ah, no. Thank you, Mr. Wengren, thank you ever so kindly. Here, sir, a pair of shillings for your kindness. What would I have done without your courtesy in watching my girls for me?"

"Not at all, sir. A pleasure. A pair of fine girls they are. I couldn't accept payment for wot we done. It were a favor I done for a good friend, sir."

"Won't you consider letting me buy you a pie? The pie man is sure to bring his wares by before the show."

"Couldn't even consider eatin' another baker's wares, Squire. But I'm much obliged for the kind offer."

The squire chuckled. "Forgive me. I forgot for a moment. Of course there are no pies quite like yours, I'll grant. Tell you what. Bring us some at the manor tomorrow. Enough for my family's dinner. That'll help our cook to decide what we'll have for dinner, won't it? Our Myrtle usually does the buying for us, of course, so I'm not familiar with the fare. Ten shillings do it?"

"Oh, that's more than enough, Squire. Too much."

"Well, then, consider bringing me the best of your lot, and I'll consider it a bargain," the squire said, handing him the ten shillings.

"You're generous, sir. I thank you. I thank you very kindly."

The baker withdrew to join his family.

"Sir?" Roseanne said.

"Yes, Roseanne?"

"I'll find chairs for us. We have them in the van. I always watch from there." She pointed to an area to the right of center stage, a space unoccupied by the makeshift benches for paying spectators. "It's where I sit." Her voice carried a note of infantile importance. She was admitting them into her world of personal privilege. She scurried to the family caravan and came back struggling with two small collapsible chairs. She quickly put the chairs in place and then returned to the van for another pair. When she had arranged them, it was clear that the space was not adequate for all four chairs, the last two too far to the right of the stage for a proper view of the action.

"I'll sit on the last chair," Roseanne offered grandly. "I've already seen the show, so it won't make any difference if I miss some of it tonight."

"No, I'll sit there," said the squire. I'm much taller than you, and if I'm off to the side, I will be less likely to block the view for those sitting behind. Matter of courtesy. You sit next to me, Miss Roseanne, then Lydia, and Catherine can occupy the first chair. Don't you think?"

Roseanne smiled broadly and nodded. By the time they had settled themselves in their none-too-comfortable places, the curtain opened and the show began.

The squire loved the show as much as his daughters did, perhaps more. It brought back the days of his own childhood, before his taste for professional competence evolved and he could laugh at the unsophisticated slap-stick comedy and traditional Punch and Judy. The actors were surprisingly competent and prepared. Roseanne announced proudly, in an eager whisper, "That's me mum," when the principal actress made her first entrance. The squire observed that she was still a very handsome woman, now a bit plumper, most likely, than when she began her career, but still quite fetching, with healthy black hair, vibrant enthusiasm and dark eyes that changed in intensity with every mood demanded of her role. Her colorful costume added to her charm. Roseanne watched her almost worshipfully, and the squire's daughters seemed lost, utterly absorbed in the new world unfolding before them.

"And that's me dad," said Roseanne as the querulous Punch appeared in the traditional *commedia dell'arte* costume, his slender, well-formed legs showing to advantage in his tights, and his remarkable baritone, a bit raspy but not unpleasant, dominating his scenes.

After the show, the squire picked up his chair and reached for Roseanne's. She protested, "I can carry them back. I brought them."

"I know, and I'm very grateful to you. I should very much like to be the one to return them to your caravan, and if your parents are there, I should like to tell them how thoroughly I enjoyed their work."

She beamed. "All right," she conceded.

The squire carried two of the chairs, and his daughters each carried her own. Mr. Withers had not yet returned to his van, but his wife met the group graciously, as vivacious off stage as on. Roseanne seemed pleased beyond words.

"Roseanne, I don't believe you've given me the pleasure of knowing who your friends are, have you, dear?"

"Oh, sorry. This is Catherine, and this is Lydia. But I don't know no more..."

"*Any* more, dear," cautioned Mrs. Withers.

"*Any* more...than that."

"I'm Edward Smirthwaite, madam," the squire proffered. "I must tell you how grateful I am that your delightful daughter fell in with my girls while I was attempting to procure a place for us to watch your remarkable show."

"Why thank you, Mr. Smirthwaite. I am Gwyneth Withers, Roseanne's mother. You know that, of course. You won't find my name on any of our bills. I was named for a famous region in Wales, but the name would create headaches for an actress who would not welcome idle questions. My stage name is Pauline Evans. Evans is my maiden name."

"So pleased, madam...Mrs. Withers. So pleased and so grateful to your daughter for befriending mine. Thanks to her, we sat comfortably through the whole show with very good position."

"Comfortably?" Mrs. Withers's laugh tinkled like thin crystal breaking. "Those chairs would inflict cramps on a jellyfish. You couldn't have been comfortable. Or well-positioned, either."

"I assure you, it was most pleasant. Much more than trying to watch standing at the rear of tonight's crowd."

"Only a gentleman, and a kindly one, could turn such hardship as you must have felt into an evening of pleasure. Thank you. I am pleased that you enjoyed our show."

"Not only the show. Your daughter's company, besides providing us access to your work, was charming. My girls seem to have taken to her quite with abandon."

"Roseanne has a venturesome spirit, Mr. Smirthwaite. I confess—quite shamelessly, as you can see—she provides us with both concern and great comfort. The concern is her energy, her endless projects, proposals, and wildly imaginative games and stories, and the comfort is in the sweetness of her disposition all the while she is worrying us with her mischief. I would be quite lost without my Rose." As she spoke, she caressed her daughter's hair and Roseanne smiled radiantly. The free expression between them touched the squire.

"Your child is obviously well schooled in manners and diction."

"Just in elementary courtesy and basic understanding, Mr. Smirthwaite. That's as far as her education can reach at the moment. We are on the road as often as weather will allow, and my time and preparation as her teacher are severely limited. She knows how to read and reads all she can, but we have few books."

"Yet her diction . . ."

"Oh, that." Mrs. Withers laughed. "I'll tell you: My father is a hard-working Welsh collier and will never have more than the barest income for his family's necessities, and I came along—the only girl in a family of seven children. And girls, as you know, are unfit for work down the pits and I complicated matters by having my head always in the clouds and a troublesome stubborn streak. I'm sure I was more a millstone than a contributor in my family. And then I met a troupe of traveling players and fell in love with the idea of becoming an actress. My family was horrified, but I had also fallen in love with young Robert Withers, the son of the troupe's director. We saw each other once or twice every season, quite enough to pledge our undying love to each other just before running home to supper. He fed my ambition with tales of their travels, the romantic notions of adventure in great cities, and the beguiling promise of fame and riches—and a life with him forever. I ran away with him. Now he is the director of our troupe, and we have fulfilled many of my dreams, though great cities have ugly tenements and filthy corners. Travel requires more strength than one can muster at times and soon becomes tiresome. And we won't speak of riches. We have seen none of those. Life with Robert has its challenges as well, but we are still together; and the fruit of our union is this one." She touched Roseanne's cheek. "She shares my weakness for the theater, and I have taught her what I myself had to learn. One cannot be an actress and speak like a miner's daughter or a milkmaid. We work daily on her diction, and I expect greater things from her than I have achieved."

"Ah," the squire responded. "If she is as successful with her audiences as she has been in captivating my daughters, her future is assured. Good heavens, what if she persuaded my girls to become actresses! I'm afraid my wife would suffer apoplexy at the thought!"

Mrs. Withers laughed again, filling the air with bells. "Really, Mr. Smirthwaite, worse things could happen."

"Forgive me, Mrs. Withers. I confess, your presence and your daughter's appealing ways are ample proof. If all actresses had your hospitable charm and your daughter's generous cheeriness, the world would have to consider yours the ablest of professions. You have given us a most unforgettable afternoon, and . . ." With a sudden dawning in his expression, he reached quickly for the watch in his waistcoat pocket. "I say, I believe I have overlooked the time. Armand was to return for us at least an hour ago. Probably wondering what could be the delay, poor chap."

"Armand?" Mrs. Withers asked.

"My coachman, madam. Dependable fellow. He'll be waiting with shortened patience by now, I should think."

That might have been true under usual circumstances, but when the squire and his daughters finally reached Eccleston Square, they found Armand in playfully earnest conversation with one of the troupe's actresses, showing not the slightest impatience with their delay. In fact, he appeared a bit reluctant to terminate his pleasant discourse as he found it necessary to help Lydia and Carolyn, now quite exhausted, into the carriage where they fell asleep before the horses had fully turned in the direction of the manor house. Night had begun to fall, and shortly down the road, Armand stopped the carriage to light the side lamps before continuing homeward. Suddenly Lydia's shrill cry shattered the silence inside the carriage.

"Odd and bossy!"

The squire came awake. "What? What?"

"My bracelet! I've lost my bracelet! It's gone! I had it, I know I did. It's the one from Grandmother . . ."

"You wore Grandmother's bracelet?" Catherine asked.

"You knew I had it on. I put it on this morning. You saw me!"

"I didn't think you'd wear it to come to the Square, did I? You said you returned it to the safe. Mother will be furious with you."

"Well, she said Grandmother left it to me, and I would get it when I was older. I just wanted to . . ."

"You wore that? The emerald bracelet?" asked the squire.

"Yes, but it is mine, isn't it? So I . . ."

"So you felt entitled to wear it without permission, is that it?"

Lydia's chin trembled as she gave a confessional nod. The squire's face struggled between severity and sympathy. Finally he sighed. "Ah, Lydia. What do you suppose we'll do when you mother discovers it's missing? No point in going back to find it now. I don't suppose you can remember where you might have been when you lost it? Well, no, of course you can't. Did you take it off at some point?"

"I . . . I don't think so. The clasp wasn't very tight, and I had to fasten it a couple of times."

"Hm. You should have given it to me. I'd have put it in my pocket and we wouldn't have to be concerned about how upset your mother will be. I think you have been told that it belonged first to your great, great grandmother."

"But Grandmother said that I could have it when I . . ."

"When you reached eighteen, my dear, and you're hardly that old today, are you? So taking it without permission was not honest, was it?"

Her misery allowed for no response.

"We can wait until morning, but then you will have to explain everything to your mother."

"Couldn't you . . . ?"

"Ah, no, child. Am I the one who lost the bracelet?"

"No, but. . ."

"Who lost it, Lydia?"

"I did."

"Well then, who should own responsibility?"

Silence. Doleful and disconsolate.

"We'll say nothing about it until morning. I dare say your mother is probably too tired to hear of our woes tonight." His voice dropped to a rueful murmur. "She wasn't keen on my taking you to the Square, which won't make matters easier."

Catherine and the squire were dozing again by the time the carriage reached the manor house, but Lydia's wretchedness held her hostage. Mrs. Smirthwaite, impatiently awaiting their arrival, ushered the girls to their bedroom without ceremony, and Lydia was grateful for a measure of reprieve, though she knew it amounted to a mere postponement. Catherine was already asleep, too exhausted to mention the bracelet. Youth and fatigue won out over Lydia's anxiety as well, as merciful slumber absorbed her and put the matter aside for the night.

But morning refused to be denied, and Lydia's problem asserted itself again when the maid woke the girls to announce breakfast.

"Did you tell Mother about the bracelet?" Catherine inquired.

"No," Lydia responded with rather surly dismissal.

But Catherine would brook no dismissal. "You'll have to tell her."

Lydia fancied that Catherine's voice carried a note of triumph, a wicked anticipation of the impending crisis.

Squire Smirthwaite was talking quietly with his wife at the table, explaining all they had done but avoiding any mention of

Lydia's bracelet. His enthusiasm with their adventure elicited no corresponding response from his redoubtable spouse who, in fact, seemed a bit nettled that he had had the temerity to enjoy himself. When the girls appeared, the conversation slowed to a halt, and the squire cleared his throat and said, "Lydia, I believe you have something to tell your mother."

Lydia squared her shoulders and surprised both the squire and Catherine with a straightforward and complete account of her delinquency in having worn the bracelet she regarded as her own and her misfortune in having lost it.

Mrs. Smirthwaite's reaction would have satisfied consummate obduracy. First she paled, then gathered her wits to rail, rave, and revile, chastising Lydia first for her indefensible breach of propriety, then her husband for his faulty judgment and his irresponsible plebeian taste. The very idea, ushering his daughters into the shoddy atmosphere of unwashed townsfolk and particularly a troupe of itinerant actors. And the word *actors* she spat out as though a wasp had sat on her tongue.

Squire Smirthwaite endured the vituperation calmly for what seemed to Lydia a long time, and finally, his demeanor still unaltered, he said firmly but quietly, "Enough. If the bracelet had thrice the value you place upon it, it would not be worth all this lather. Armand and I will return to the Square and make inquiries. And if we fail to find it, madam, the world will still turn as it always has."

Mrs. Smirthwaite sputtered on. "You'll never find it now. Those people, those *actors*, have it. They stole it, I have no doubt. It's what comes with their ilk. That snippet of a girl who pretended to be so friendly saw the jewels and found the way to pinch them."

Lydia flinched. She had never before heard the vulgar expression "pinch them" in her mother's ample lexical arsenal. She almost laughed but saved herself in time. She could ill afford to snicker at anything her mother was saying at a time like this. She vaguely recognized the expression as her mother's way of ridiculing the people she imagined would use such language. But Lydia could not dismiss the thought of the utter injustice in it. Roseanne, she knew, was innocent of any misdemeanor, or even the thought of it, and she was being accused of theft, without being present to hear the accusation and thus deprived of any opportunity to deny it, simply because she happened to belong to a lower social class and therefore must not be trusted and even deserved to be blamed. No other evidence seemed to be required.

Lydia was told to go to her room and await her sentence, which her mother would pronounce as soon as she could devise something severe enough to fit the crime. Alone there, Lydia was almost surprised to discover that she really did not care what punishment might follow; what disturbed her was the thought of Roseanne, so quickly her friend, accused of a theft that was no theft at all, arbitrarily relegated to a category of delinquency with no opportunity to defend herself, and Lydia knew that no defense could be summoned that would placate her mother or change her views.

She tried to assuage her agitation with a book, but that attempt faltered in less than an hour. She tried to rest, lying on the bed, but abandoned that measure and sat on the edge, wondering how long her banishment would last before the next phase of punishment would begin. She heard a noise from somewhere outside. She listened more carefully. It appeared to be sounds of a horse being moved from stable to carriage, and those sounds drew her to the window, where she saw that Armand, as she had imagined, was supervising the stable boys' hooking of traces to carriage. The process completed, Squire Smirthwaite took his place in the carriage, Armand took his, and the carriage drove away. Lydia was sure they were on their way to recover, if possible, what she had lost. She sighed deeply and returned dejected to her desk and retrieved her book again, but her reading was again sporadic and without concentration and lasted less than an hour. It was interrupted by another sound, the sound of a horse approaching. Again she scurried to the window in time to see her father spring from his light carriage and hurry toward the house. In the distance, Lydia could see a slower conveyance approaching. It appeared to be a caravan, like the one she had visited the day before. She returned in some perplexity to her book. Her banishment would not allow her any part of whatever was unfolding outside.

Shortly, Catherine burst through the door.

"Roseanne's coming! She's bringing the bracelet!"

"What? What did you say?"

"Father met them on the road. They were on the way here. Roseanne found your bracelet and is bringing it to you. She wants to give it to you herself."

"Roseanne . . . She found it? Where?"

"I don't know. But they're coming! Father talked to them. . . Oh, you'll get the story when they get here. Come on!"

"Mother told me I had to stay put."

"But . . . Don't you want to see Roseanne?"

"Of course, but I can't, can I?"

"Well . . . Oh, come on! Mother won't even remember. Come on!"

Lydia needed no further urging. She sprang up and flew away with Catherine in a blur of release, mingled with lingering apprehension.

When the girls, scampering hand-in-hand across the garden, reached the stable yard where the stable hands had directed the Withers' van, Roseanne and her parents had already descended and were in earnest conversation with the squire and Mrs. Smirthwaite. It was clear to Lydia that her mother intended no more acceptance than social courtesy would allow. Her face wore a forced smile and studied aloofness. A glance in Lydia's direction gave her to understand that her mother was not pleased that she had left her room without permission. When Roseanne, catching sight of Catherine and Lydia, rushed to them and hugged them with unrestrained affection, Mrs. Smirthwaite paled at the unmitigated audacity, the sheer impudence of the girl, hardly above the status of gypsies who live on the road and sleep in caravans. Her smile, such as it was, faded and her brow creased in lines of rigid severity. What galled her most was that her daughters, especially Lydia, were behaving with equal abandon, as though the matter of quality had never been taught them. Lydia was actually weeping! Moreover, the squire himself welcomed "those people" as warmly as if they were social equals, which left Mrs. Smirthwaite wordless.

Lydia and Catherine lost no time in initiating a tour of the premises with Roseanne, from garden to stable, dovecote to meadow, carriage house to parlor. Mrs. Smirthwaite excused herself to attend to an urgent domestic matter which she did not stop to explain.

The squire chatted amiably and graciously with Roseanne's parents, showing them the stables and gardens. At length they protested that they must be moving on. The detour they had taken to return the lost bracelet had put them hours behind the other members of their troupe, and they were scheduled to play the next day in another town. They found it necessary to interrupt Roseanne's adventure with her new-found friends and insist that she come forthwith. Her protests never reached the point of tantrum, but they were shrill and persuasive enough to elicit promises from her parents that on their return the next year, or perhaps sooner, they would be pleased to entertain the squire and his girls as their special guests for their performances, with a guaranteed seat for them in an advantageous position for viewing. In his turn, the squire extended his own invitation for them to appear any time at the manor, and he assured them that they could expect to dine with him and his family. Fortunately, Mrs. Smirthwaite was not present to witness the arrangement.

Lydia watched the Withers' van grow smaller as distance diminished it and then followed the squire and Catherine inside the house with some misgivings, and as she expected, her mother was there waiting to scold her once more for her carelessness in losing the bracelet. When the squire was able to quiet her and inform her of his invitation to "those people" to return any time, she was livid.

"I should think you would welcome them gladly," ventured the squire mildly. "They put themselves to no small inconvenience to return Lydia's bracelet, and now it's safe again. The very least we can do is show a modicum of gratitude. Besides, I find them quite delightful."

Mrs. Smirthwaite could not manage a satisfactory rejoinder; she was clearly outnumbered. She merely launched an offended "Well!" into the air as though she had been struck by a flying dust mop, and then clung to her dignity by flouncing out of their company.

Lydia still held the bracelet Roseanne had returned to her, turning it over in her hands. Then she took a resolute breath and followed her mother to the bedroom where she was sure her mother had taken indignant refuge. She knocked softly.

"Leave me to myself, if you please," came the voice from the other side of the door. Its owner was no doubt expecting her husband.

"I want to give you the bracelet," Lydia said a bit tremulously. A long silence followed, and then Lydia heard the bolt sliding and the knob turning. She held up the bracelet, and the light from the window made the emeralds glow like dew on bright green spring leaves.

"I'm sorry I lost it. I'm sorry I took it without asking."

Her mother's face softened as she took the bracelet and touched Lydia's cheek gently, a passing caress.

"I know you meant no harm, child. But the bracelet is an heirloom and very valuable. We respect those things, my dear. I didn't mean to be harsh. You may hold it again from time to time, and when you reach the age . . ."

"I don't want it. Please give it to Catherine."

"But . . . She will get the necklace . . ."

"She's older, and anyway I don't want it anymore." Lydia turned and walked away, again leaving Mrs. Smirthwaite wordless, perplexed, and chafing at her daughter's churlishness.

No subsequent entreaty could persuade Lydia to change her mind. She had definitively rejected the bracelet as a gift intended for her, since, as she reasoned, she was deemed unfit to possess it and was unwilling to abide the years that would give her requisite maturity. Mrs. Smirthwaite fretted silently over the view her mother, who had bestowed the gift in the first place, would surely take if she learned of Lydia's rejection. She decided it would be best not to mention the matter and restored the bracelet to the jewel nest in the family safe.

Twice the following year, the Withers passed through Eccleston, stopping to visit Squire Smirthwaite's manor house in response to his warm invitation, but more urgent than his invitation were Roseanne's pleas to allow her time with Lydia and Catherine. They in turn responded so eagerly to Roseanne that even Mrs. Smirthwaite, without fully condoning her daughters' forming close bonds with the likes of "those minstrel people," bowed to their wishes with aloof tolerance. Unable to bend her husband's liberal views toward her own aristocratic exclusiveness, and reluctantly recognizing that her daughters would not consent to forego their pleasure in Roseanne's ready wit, creative schemes, and exciting games and projects, she more or less held her peace, but it was an uneasy peace.

The second year, the travelers' performance in the square involved extensive preparation for new material they had added to the stock *comedia dell'arte* fare. The Smirthwaite girls, learning that those preparations would take all of one day and part of another, implored so soulfully that Roseanne be allowed to spend the day and overnight with them that Roseanne's parents, with the squire's hearty approval, consented. Mrs. Smirthwaite, unable to find anything concretely unseemly in the arrangement, nodded her own reluctant consent. The girls were ecstatic, and Lydia, in the swirl of her excitement, contrived to have Armand carry a note to the Hamilton manor to invite Emmeline, her closest school friend, to join them, making it a celebration that would never fade from memory.

It was also during that delightfully spontaneous occasion that Lydia observed a pale fragility in Roseanne that she had not noticed before. She was as brightly original, as quick, clever, and cheerful as ever, but she lost energy easily and coughed frequently. Lydia wondered if Roseanne's malady could be similar to the lung weakness that she herself had always had to endure. She almost questioned her about it when on a trek through the fields Roseanne found it necessary to rest on a bank while the others continued with their play. She did not stop smiling and commenting, and stayed in rhythm with the others' activities, and soon she arose to join them again. Lydia lost the chance to question her and then shrugged the matter off, ascribing Roseanne's symptoms to a likely cold.

The following year, the Withers' stay was much shorter, limiting Roseanne to a brief afternoon with the Smirthwaite girls and Emmeline Hamilton. Lydia noticed a marked difference now in Roseanne, who had lost weight and whose energy had dropped to a level of listlessness that Lydia would have thought impossible. The girls spent their time chatting and reading, and as usual it was all very pleasant, but clearly Roseanne was no longer capable of the more strenuous running, climbing, and exploring they had enjoyed a scant year earlier.

The squire ordered Armand to prepare his carriage to take Roseanne into Eccleston, obviating the necessity of her parents' traveling out of their way to fetch her. Lydia begged to go with Roseanne and return with Armand. The squire had no objection but deferred to his wife, who wanted to refuse, but seeing the familiar flare of determination in Lydia's eyes yielded with the rather peevish conciliation, "Oh, very well, if you must, but I will never understand your need to lower yourself to that child's common level. You seem determined always to diminish yourself."

Lydia answered with a rather saucy nod that was meant to convey gratitude but turned into a gesture just short of impudence. She walked away before her anger could betray her.

How could anyone imagine that it was lowering oneself to seek the company and even emulate the qualities of a person so obviously superior? Lydia had never known a brighter, more clever, or more interesting person than Roseanne Withers. No one could justly regard her as inferior, either in conduct or integrity, not to mention intelligence. But, since argument would only aggravate without ever gaining a point where her mother was concerned, she chose silence and boarded the carriage, sitting next to Roseanne in vexed confusion, which lasted less than a mile. Time with Roseanne was too precious to waste on sullenness.

But in that mile, her mind argued with her mother. She remembered Matthew Warren, her father's steward, whom she heard her father describe as the finest man he knew. What puzzled her as a child was that her father knew many men, most of them with rank and high connection, and Matthew held no social status beyond his high rank among the household servants and in her father's esteem. Among her father's acquaintances was Squire Farnsworth-Braden, whom everyone revered. He took lively interest in children's education, working closely with the vicar and the parochial school, often dispensing financial aid and supplying other needs for the worthy poor. She knew how her father admired him and yet did not favor him as highly as he favored Matthew Warren. If Matthew was the best man her father knew, why was he not a baron, a count, a duke, or even a king?

That question, put to her mother, evoked an impatient dismissal with the crisp reminder that blood alone determined rank.

Matthew Warren had been Squire Smirthwaite's steward for as long as Lydia could remember, and when he died, the squire was disconsolate. Matthew had served superbly, but the squire regarded him as his confidant and companion as well. His word had always bound him, and no man could have budged him from his duty or his commitments, be they trivial or essential. After his funeral, the squire bestowed a lavish endowment upon his widow, and Lydia overheard him explaining to Mrs. Smirthwaite that Matthew's large family had little more than the competence required for necessities.

"Blasted shame. Best man I ever knew."

Mrs. Smirthwaite sighed.

"I know, my dear. But we do what we're born to, don't we?"

―――

The Smirthwaite carriage met the troupe's entourage, as expected, just out of Eccleston en route to their next engagement. Mrs. Withers, who on this occasion had been reluctant to allow even a brief separation from Roseanne, showed what might have been perceived as overweening concern for her.

"I'm fine, Mum," Roseanne assured.

Lydia suddenly sensed that what she had noticed in Roseanne's altered strength and energy was not a passing malady but a chronic condition, but she had no opportunity to confirm her suspicions. The troupe was in a hurry to move on. Mrs. Withers embraced Lydia, impelled by a worried wistfulness, a frightening urgency, but she broke abruptly away and mounted the conveyance to sit next to her husband as the caravan rolled on. Lydia climbed into her own carriage to return home.

Early the next summer, on a bright day in June, Lydia spotted a vehicle of unmistakable familiarity approaching the manor house. Her heart quickened and her cheeks flushed. It seemed to her that those wheels must be shod with lead; they seemed to move the caravan too slowly. She scurried to alert Catherine and the squire that the Withers were approaching. They joined her to greet their visitors when they drew into the courtyard and were met with Mr. Withers' doleful expression and Mrs. Withers' wan smile. Roseanne was not with them.

Mrs. Withers descended wordlessly from the van and gathered both Lydia and Catherine in a soulful embrace. Her tears were her only utterance. Mr. Withers, as he took the squire's hand, explained that they had buried Roseanne two weeks back. Tuberculosis had claimed her.

Lydia sank to her knees, weeping, the only response she could find for her confusion, outrage, shock, and grief. Catherine stood next to her, sobbing. Mrs. Withers found her voice: "We hoped she could—she wanted to see you again, but . . ." She took a breath. "We couldn't manage to get here before . . ."

"I had no idea," sputtered the squire. "Was she hospitalized?"

"The doctor saw her, but he said it was too late. We should have seen him sooner, he said."

"If I had known, we could have given her medical attention."

"Traveling players don't have much knowledge of such things or means to change them," said Mr. Withers. "We kept expecting her to improve, but when she started coughing blood, we knew—and we knew too late."

The Withers declined the squire's offer of refreshment. They were pressed to continue their journey. Lydia never saw them again. But years and the varied experiences they brought could not erase her memory of them.

Two

"Willa's leaving, Henry," Lydia informed, showing some petulance.

"Not too surprising. You told me she had a follower. Marrying him, is she?"

"She told me this morning."

Henry lit his pipe. The smell of tobacco, so common and homey, at the moment seemed inexplicably irritating.

"I'd like to help her get on," Henry said, blowing smoke toward the window. "Some small parting gift, what? Poor lass can't count on much of a dowry."

"No, I suppose not. What are we going to do without her, though? Horse Stone House is going to seem larger than ever without my maid."

"Larger than ever? Less than a quarter the size of your mother's little castle, I'd guess."

"Yes, but Mother has an army at her command, and all I had was Willa."

"There's Mrs. Folsum, don't forget."

"Oh, I won't forget. She's a cook, not a maid, as she would readily remind you should you try to impose maid's duty upon her."

"Well, we can advertise. Shouldn't be hard to find a replacement."

Lydia bit her lip, scowling slightly. "No," she announced with sudden decision. "I'm going to ask Mother for Madge. I brought her to Mother in the first place, didn't I? And trained her. Did most of it myself."

"Yes, so you've told me."

It was five years ago . . .

On invitation from their cousin Alice Kirkham, who lived in Liverpool, Lydia and Catherine Smirthwaite, accompanied by their mother who welcomed the opportunity to visit her sister, joined Alice for some shopping and leisure.

On one of their pleasurable excursions, the three girls visited a fashionable section of the city, and emerging from a rather stylish dress shop, laughing and chatting, they failed to pay proper attention as they crossed the busy street where a carriage rounded upon them, nearly striking Catherine and spattering mud on all three. Catherine shrieked. The carriage driver cast them a scathing glare and cursed.

"Bleedin' near got it, din't ye? Serve yer right, not lookin' abaht afore crossin'."

The girls stood, mouths agape, speechless and mud-spattered as the carriage lurched away. Alice had a smudge on her cheek and looked on the verge of tears, the cab driver's crude abuse still raging through her sensibilities.

Lydia began to laugh.

"What in the world . . . ?" Catherine gasped, with a look almost as baleful as the one the carriage driver had cast them. "What's so funny?"

"We are. Look at us!" She brushed her hand over her dress, and instead of helping matters smeared the mud more broadly over the fabric. It brought another burst of laughter. "We look worse than a crew of chimney sweeps!"

Alice began to wail, and Catherine shot another irascible glance at Lydia, who turned her head to hide her amusement, but her heaving shoulders betrayed her. When Catherine looked squarely at Alice, who had abandoned her dignity to anguish, the scene burst upon her as well and she too began to giggle. Alice wailed the louder, and the two sisters almost collapsed. It took several minutes for them to gain a modicum of control and try to comfort their forlorn cousin.

"Come on, now, it's not so bad. Rather a jolly surprise, wasn't it?" Catherine cajoled, putting her arm about Alice's waist.

Lydia joined her on Alice's opposite side, and the three began walking down a street quite unfamiliar, Alice still nurturing her indignation. They walked for several minutes before the two sisters managed to tease out a smile from her, and even then her face seemed prepared to suffer a relapse. They walked on, the sisters affecting buoyancy, Alice relenting by degrees, and soon all three were quite cheerful again.

"Where are we going?" Catherine ventured.

Lydia looked around. So did Alice. Lydia shrugged. Alice was the one who began to laugh. "Now we don't even know where we are!" she chortled, and finally all three were laughing together.

"I don't recognize anything," Alice confessed.

"What does it matter?" Lydia suggested. "At worst, we can follow our steps back to where we turned the corner, can't we? And we can always hail a hansom and rely on the driver to return us to your house, Alice."

They took another turn to follow a new street and walked on, a little inflamed now with the desire to explore. But soon the smells and sounds of squalor, the suspicious, resentful glances cast them by the local denizens brought them to realize they were quite out of their element. Alice paled slightly.

"We're in . . . I'm sure this is a tenement district." The awe and fear in her voice told her cousins much more than the words.

"What . . . what does that mean?" Lydia asked.

"I don't know. But I would never be permitted to come to such a place. Mother will be furious. We . . . we need to . . ."

"Oh, we can find our way back," Lydia said lightly. "We'll probably have to. I don't see any hansoms for hire here."

"Or carriages or guides or . . . or friends," Catherine observed ruefully.

They continued on, tentatively, curious but fearful. As they passed a dark alleyway, Alice's steps grew hesitant.

"Let's ... ah ... let's go back now," she suggested.

The other two nodded, and they turned around, again passing the dark alleyway, now in the opposite direction. A few steps beyond, Lydia felt a tug on her skirt. She controlled the impulse to scream but could not stifle a gasp that drew the other girls' attention. A child in a tattered dress, soil smudges over her face and elsewhere, stood looking with imploring eyes into Lydia's face. She had emerged from the alleyway. Her small frame looked younger than her face, and none of the young ladies would have hazarded to guess her exact age. The face might have been pretty had it the grace of a recent washing, though it was much too thin, with a pinched look about the mouth and the nose a bit too long.

"Flahrs, ma'am?" She held a few drooping violets. "Buy me flahrs?" The hungry eyes never left Lydia's, as though the others were not present at all.

Quite suddenly, from the shadows of the same alleyway, another figure darted and struck the violets from the girl's hand.

"Ar, what're yeeou doin' 'ere? In't your patch. This 'ere's my territ'ry."

"I picked them flahrs in the commons, I did. No one as owns the flahrs what grows in the commons," the girl answered.

"Don't matter. This in't yer place, no matter as yer picked 'em in the commons or stole 'em from me. Yer got no rights 'ere."

Lydia and her companions had found no voice even to express their surprise. The new girl, larger by half than the trembling little interloper, suddenly dealt her a resounding slap. The victim shrieked, and the larger girl had her hand raised for a second blow when Lydia seized her arm.

"Stop that! Stop it this instant!"

The larger girl did not deliver the threatened blow but turned sullen eyes on Lydia. She measured about the same in height and no doubt weighed more.

"She ain't one of us. This in't 'er patch and she 'as no call ter sell nuffink 'ere."

"That does not excuse your viciousness. She's smaller and weaker than you are. Leave her."

The girl made no move to retreat.

"I said leave her! And do it at once!"

The girl's eyes held anger and resentment, like an enraged badger deprived of its kill. "This in't your place neither. Got no call to come 'ere wiv vem fine cloves and talkin' like a bloomin' nob."

"That's as may be, but understand me, you will not attack this child again. Now off with you before I find a constable."

The girl's withdrawal had no submission in it, only a grudging acknowledgment of superior opposition and a churlish hostility in her eyes.

The little girl dusted herself off, shaken but tearless. She gave an awkward nod of her head that might have served as a reverence. "Thank yer, ma'am. Could I . . . um . . . walk wiv yer a bit? Can't stay 'ere now. She'll be layin' fer me wen ye've gone."

"Where do you live?" Alice ventured.

"Not nowhere now. They took me mum away, and I ain't seen 'er these three days. I used to live over there." She gestured toward a distant row of tenements.

"Who took her?" Lydia demanded.

"Don't know, ma'am. She were too sick t' work and she coun't pay 'er part o' the rent. She's gone. She ain't comin' back."

"Surely she will. She wouldn't leave you like this."

"She don't 'ave no choosin' of it. She ain't comin' back."

"We'll take you back to your . . . where you live," Lydia said lamely.

"Can't. They won't let me in cos I don't 'ave nuffin' to pay rent wif neither."

"Three days, child? Who feeds you?" Lydia asked, her voice betraying the strong suspicion that she already knew the answer.

"I eats wot I can find. Last night I ate wot Miles Fernley 'ad for me. Miles minds the pub as is on the corner where I used to live. 'E was goin' to chuck it in the bin, 'e was. Food as someone left on 'is plate. I ate it wen Miles looked away. 'E's good to look away, is Miles. I ain't 'ad nuffin' today. Maybe wen Miles closes up . . ."

"We can't leave this child in the street," Lydia said, the imperious note of resolution in her voice.

"What can we do?" Catherine questioned. "We can hardly take her with us."

"Of course not," Lydia answered. "We couldn't be expected to let kindness overrule propriety, could we?"

They were now near the corner where they had made the fateful turn that eventually led them to the neighborhood of tenement houses. A hansom stood a little way off.

"I'm going to take that cab. You two find your own," Lydia said, seizing the dirty child's hand and pulling her along, trailing surprise and no little reluctance toward the hansom.

Catherine and Alice stood with unhinged jaws as they watched Lydia engage the driver and practically lift the child into the seat, the driver himself protesting. Lydia's sharp rebuke silenced him, and the hansom drove away.

"What's your name?" Lydia asked almost tenderly.

"Madge."

"Madge. Madge . . . ?"

"Showett, ma'am."

"How old are you, Madge Showett?"

"Thirteen, ma'am."

Lydia almost gasped but managed merely to nod. She had guessed the girl to be much younger. She was a mere three years younger than Lydia herself. Slowly, Lydia began to scheme. Myrtle, their housemaid in Eccleston, had a "follower," and by now it was known that he would surely speak for her soon.

When they reached the Kirkham mansion, Lydia had a time convincing the butler to let her in with the dirty waif, but Lydia prevailed and then attacked the problem she knew she would have with her mother. First, she had the housemaid scrub little Madge until her skin looked rosy. By then, Catherine and Alice had returned, and together they procured food from the kitchen over the cook's mild protest. Madge ate wolfishly, overcoming her shyness in the grand house. Then they dressed her in some of Alice's little sister's cast-off clothes. Finally, Lydia explained to Catherine her plans for Madge. At first Catherine protested, but eventually she bowed to Lydia's persuasions. Together they approached their mother, armed with Lydia's independent spiritedness and both girls' compassionate resolve.

The timing was fortuitous. Otherwise they would likely have suffered defeat, but Mrs. Smirthwaite, with no great affinity for inconvenience, listened when her daughters explained that Madge, now thirteen, was of age for service and she could be trained before Myrtle, their present maid, left their employ. Notwithstanding Mrs. Smirthwaite's misgiving, Madge became a part of the Smirthwaite household retinue. The arrangement offered many challenges at first, beginning with Myrtle's resentment and Mrs. Smirthwaite's skepticism, but Mrs. Gradwell, the cook, already quite critical of Myrtle's growing laziness and carelessness, took the new girl's part, while Lydia and Catherine enlisted her help quite shamelessly, and Marvin the butler's as well, and together they covered Madge's mistakes and tutored her carefully prior to each pressing responsibility.

They made her appear particularly competent when Mrs. Smirthwaite, in a panic over a dinner party she had planned with social peers and other people of connection, began to bewail Myrtle's absence just when she was most needed and complained of awkward little Madge's lack of experience and aplomb. Madge's allies drilled her mercilessly, covering every move and every possible situation, and apparently they succeeded. Madge gave a flawless performance, and the evening's success obliged Mrs. Smirthwaite, to her credit, to express her pleasure and even confess that she might have been a bit hasty in her previous judgments.

The evening over, Lydia and Catherine collapsed for two days from nervous exhaustion. By then Mrs. Gradwell had developed such affection for Madge that she found herself struggling not to let her partiality show among the other household help, and Marvin did not even bother to hide *his* partiality. Madge, for her part, began to acquire a sense of belonging and a pride in her service, with an almost worshipful affection for Lydia and a strong but lesser regard for Catherine. By the time Lydia married and moved to Horse Stone, Catherine had long since made her own nest, and Madge, though beholden to Mrs. Gradwell and Marvin, felt disconsolate, and it showed in her face, her sluggish movements, her every expression, though she was careful always not to do sloppy work. Mrs. Smirthwaite scolded her, and she mended her behavior only in that she kept herself erect and moved with summary alacrity when bidden. Clearly, the core of her cheeriness had withered, her smiles scarce and wan.

Lydia, unwittingly blessed with the circumstance of Madge's drooping spirits, approached her mother when Willa left her employ. She was quite ready to remind her mother of how Madge had come to them in the first place and was quite willing to plead and cajole. Her mother, already softened by Madge's unhappiness, listened, smiling to herself. She was perhaps still learning that in the face of Lydia's resolve, one is best served by capitulation anyway, and any delay would merely postpone the inevitable. She interrupted her daughter with an imperious wave of her hand.

"Oh, take the girl and be gone. It's the only way to see either of you smile again."

Lydia concealed her immense pleasure and made great haste to gather Madge's meager belongings and whisk her home to Horse Stone. Once back in Lydia's service, Madge quickly recovered the bounce in her step and the glint of pleasure in her deep brown eyes. Her spirited nature addled Mrs. Folsum, the cook, but her willing response to the older woman's direction soon won the dour widow's affection—an affection never directly expressed—and acknowledged only in her sturdy defense of Madge against anyone who had the temerity to criticize or malign her. Mrs. Folsum held securely to her rank and seniority, but her severity, while never faltering, never reached the level of tyranny. Madge felt herself balanced on the pinnacle of good fortune.

When she became acquainted with others of her station, she discovered that many served in much grander circumstances, but they held little or no privilege or enjoyed no confidence with their employers, and occasionally one might suffer misuse or abuse from an adult male of the household. Moreover, a rigid hierarchy prevailed among the servants themselves, with frequent vying for position or favor and tyrannical imposition from those above them. Though their responsibilities were usually defined and duties less extensive, Madge felt herself superior because she was alone in Lydia's service, beholden only to her employers and Mrs. Folsum, whom she manipulated adroitly. More important still, she enjoyed Lydia's confidence, and slowly, Lydia taught her how to read, placing her a good notch above any average housemaid. When the babies came, Madge's duties increased, but she accepted the change just as Lydia did, as normal and expected. Lydia had less time for teaching and reading or other treasured moments alone with her, but they cared for the children together, and Madge's pleasure in the little ones increased with their stature and development. She remembered fondly her service in the Smirthwaite mansion, but her sense of belonging flourished here in the cozier confines of Horse Stone, with Lydia who had rescued her, Henry who accepted her and treated her with respectful affection, and the babies who loved her.

Three

Lydia paused unnecessarily before the fireplace. Unnecessarily. She knew she could not stay there long. Why did she bother? There was never enough time just to stand and absorb. Horse Stone House was too large for a woman with just one maid and two small children. Her tasks obliged her to move about, distance herself from that soothing flood of warmth where the fireplace yawned so comfortingly. Fire was allowed only in the parlor and withdrawing room, unless there was illness that required heat in a bedroom. As Henry often pointed out, they were hardly blessed with the means that could provide limitless fuel for all the rooms in Horse Stone House. Comfortable it may be made to be, but within reason.

She loved Horse Stone House. It was different from her childhood home, but so much dearer, like a poor cousin who wins your affection without fanfare, with the simple dignity of unvarnished quality. She did not reject her origins, even remembered them tenderly, and often thought of the vast manor house with its emblazoned elegance. It exuded ripe family tradition, from the inherited polished wood pieces—her father's desk, her mother's highboy, and countless others—the crystal chandeliers and deep-cushioned furniture, to the portraits, redolent of noble antiquity, that lined the staircase and monitored one's ascent or descent. Grandfather Smirthwaite's heavy jowls and dignified scowl and censorial expression, Grandmother Winthrop, who looked down so benignly and smiled a bit impishly, Great-grandfather Smirthwaite, slender and lithesome in his hunting attire, his gun serenely silent and his dog at rest, and all the others inspecting you and reminding you in their strident silence of their severe expectations. Lydia did not chafe at their expectations, but she could never absorb them as proprietary responsibilities exclusive to her rank. Others seemed just as capable of admirable qualities as she or her forebears.

Horse Stone House was home. No impressive progenitors to accuse, fulminate, or look down in condescending indulgence from their lofty perch in eternity. Horse Stone was not a distant reminder or a cold expectation but a comfortable now. Lydia belonged here, not because she was blessed with a particular recipe of superior blood-mingling but because she chose to make a place for herself with a husband whose blood she regarded as highly as her own, though her genealogy and connections were clearly and severely superior and her society likely to demur. Let them. She was content, and with her husband she intended to start her own canon of expectations with her own children.

Lydia heard the knock at the large front door but waited. Madge would answer it. The visitor was Emmeline Plowhurst, Lydia's kindly friend, whom she had known since she was a girl. Simple, retiring, and moderately attractive Emmeline. Well, married to Rupert Plowhurst, who wouldn't be retiring? A wonder she could manage to get his permission to come calling.

"Is your mistress in?" Lydia heard Emmeline ask.

"Yes ma'am, Mrs. Plow'urst, I'm sure. Come in, please."

Lydia moved away from the fire and stood near the table, smiling her greeting.

"Emmeline, it's grand to see you. Come sit close to the fire with me. I can't get enough of it on these cold days. It's bad enough in our green and pleasant England even when the sun shines."

Emmeline smiled. "Thank you, Lydia." She sat, folded her hands in her lap and looked uneasy, saying nothing.

"Well, as I said before, it's good to see you. Is your family well?" Lydia pursued.

"We're tolerably well, thank you. Except . . ." she shrugged, uncertain.

"Mr. Plowhurst ailing?"

"No."

"One of the children?"

"No. It's me, I guess. Lydia, I've got to talk. I don't know anyone else I'd share this with. Maybe . . ."

"What, Emmeline?"

"Maybe I'd better not. . ."

"For odd and bossy, what's the matter?"

Emmeline laughed and wiped the palms of her hands on her skirt. "Odd and bossy? I swear, Lydia, you say the strangest things."

"Oh, I suppose I do. I haven't dropped all the silly things I picked up when I was a child. Our vicar always used to say, 'Od's body.' Another silly expression, but he told us he got it from reading Shakespeare, and that was reason enough for him to use it and for the world to accept it. My sister started using it, but she couldn't get it straight; it became *odd and bossy*, and our whole family picked it up that way. It was a not-too-subtle method of making fun of our stuffy vicar. Anyway, sorry to distract you. Seems to me you had something else in mind, didn't you?"

Emmeline looked away. "I . . . it's hard."

"Madge?" Lydia called, as a thought suddenly dawned.

"Yes ma'am?" Madge answered, stepping into the doorway.

"We would like tea, please, dear. I should have remembered. You will take tea, won't you, Em?"

"Oh, I wouldn't bother."

"It's no bother. Is it, Madge?"

"No, ma'am. None at all." Madge turned and left to be about her errand.

"So now, Emmeline, back to your problem. I assume it *is* a problem. You needn't worry that I'll go blabbing it about, and if it's something you need to share, you know I'll listen."

"Yes. I know that. I know. But have I the right?"

"Right to what? To speak?"

"I mean, my husband. He might . . ."

"Mr. Plowhurst? Why should he mind? What have you done, Em?"

"Nothing. I mean . . . I've been . . . listening to a preacher. A missionary. You know how I love to read, and he gave me a book. I have to keep it hidden. I keep it under the mattress. It's not seemly, is it, to hide things from your husband?"

"Oh, Mercy, I don't know anyone who doesn't have a secret or two. A preacher, you say? What in the world . . .?"

"A missionary. He's got a new church."

"Why would you want a new church?"

"I don't know. What he said . . . Lydia, it sounds so strange, but sensible. Why would God stop talking to us? Didn't He talk to people before? The vicar says He talked with Adam and Abraham. I'm ignorant, I know, but we have the Bible and I read it. So does Rupert. He reads it to me all the time. Seems like he'd rather I didn't, as if a woman can only understand what her husband tells her, but I can read, and God did talk to men once."

"Well, yes, but that was before the Bible."

"What does that have to do with anything? Why does the Bible steal God's voice?"

"It doesn't steal God's voice, Emmeline; it *is* God's voice."

"And that means He has no more to say to us? What would keep Him from speaking now, if He wanted to?"

Madge brought in the tea, with savory little suet cakes. When Madge left, Lydia set her teacup aside.

"So, you are distressed that God no longer cares to address us. Why is that?" Lydia asked.

"No reason, except that the vicar tells us of an unchanging God, but He no longer cares to speak. It would be so comforting to know that He hasn't abandoned us. And if He is unchanging, why did He stop speaking as He used to? Isn't that a change?"

"I don't know. Has He talked to your preacher friend? Is that what you're telling me?"

"No. But He talked to a prophet in America. A man who was looking for God's church, and God came to him."

"God came . . ." she caught her breath. "Emmeline, no wonder you don't want to mention it! Mr. Plowhurst . . ."

"Lydia, he mustn't know! It would be . . ."

"I won't tell him, you know I won't. I won't tell anyone. If I didn't know you for a sane and saintly woman, I'd think you'd become deranged. Potty, as we said in school. But I won't be responsible for sending you to Bedlam for it."

"I'm not potty. I've read the book God gave the prophet, that's all. I've read it, and I believe it. I'm not taking the missionary's word for anything. I've read the book, and no man could write it. No man, Lydia, unless God showed him how!"

"And that's the book you're hiding from Mr. Plowhurst. I don't wonder. Must be quite exciting."

"Well, it is, I suppose. I feel so . . . um . . . naughty," she giggled. "I've never tried to hide anything from him before."

"Never? Don't I remember you saying you didn't intend to tell him how much you spent on your little darling's birthday gift?"

"Oh, that's not the same at all. I saved the money myself. Pennies each time I gave Nora money for food. Just pennies at a time. It took me a whole year."

"See? Everyone cheats a little that way. Even Henry gets a bit unreasonable over expenditures. But your book—now, that could be a bigger problem."

"I know. Lydia, what can I do? I can't just throw it away and pretend it's not important. I've read it, and I believe. It would be like pretending you don't believe you're eating pudding while you're eating pudding. Well, that's silly, perhaps, but you know what I mean."

"Emmeline, I have to tell you—I think you'll take it from me because you know my feelings. You know you're dear to me. You're one of the best people I know, because your heart is as innocent as your intentions are good, but your judgment—is not always flawless, is it?"

"No. No, I guess not. I am absent-minded, aren't I? And silly . . ."

"Now don't do that. If I criticize, you always put yourself down, and that's not what I want at all. I just want you to see that maybe this . . . this thing you have with this missionary . . ."

"Oh, Lydia, this missionary is a dear old thing, but not the sort one gets romantically fond of. It's what he preaches, and the book . . ."

"Yes, the book. But can't you see what I'm saying? With a little time and reason, this fancy will pass. Like the need we used to feel for dreaming of riches and happy-ever-after stories."

"No. Please don't try to make this a fancy of my immaturity. I'm trying to tell you. Really, I wanted to talk to you because of all people, you know me with all my faults and all my silliness and you know that something in me is deeper and serious. You know I'm more than a child who still dreams of 'happy ever after.' This has touched me, Lydia. Reached inside me. I can't—I won't—just give it up as a daydream. Can you judge the book *I* have read better than I can? Because you haven't read it! Judge my judgment after we're standing on the same level!"

"All right, Emmeline. Of course you're right. I haven't read the book, but what you've told me of it certainly doesn't give me great curiosity or any reassurance at all. A book from a man who says he talks to God! He's either insane or a blasphemer."

"You're judging. You tell me, 'All right, Emmeline. Of course you're right,' and then begin to tell me how wrong I am. I've read a book I believe in! And you tell me I shouldn't believe. Why can't God talk to us today?"

"Don't excite yourself. I'm sorry. It's as hard for me not to reject the book as it is for you not to defend it, but as you say, you *have* read it and I haven't."

"Will . . . will you read it, Lydia? Will you please read it so you can help me believe I'm not crazy for what I see in it?"

"I . . . hum . . . Read it? Well, no, I can't do that. I don't want . . . I'm not dissatisfied with my belief, my dear."

"I didn't think I was either. I'm not trying to convert you, Lydia. I just want someone to understand me. I want someone I can trust to tell me I'm not an immature child whose judgment is always suspect. The book is true, and I just want you to tell me I'm not daft for believing it!"

"I don't know, Em. I'd rather not get mixed up with . . ."

"With me, Lydia? Am I already judged, then? I'm the one who's read it. I'm not asking you to join Brother Kimball's church. I just want someone to tell me it's all right to believe God can still speak to us."

"Brother Kimball? He's the prophet, then, the one in America?"

"No, he's the missionary who's here trying to get people to listen. And I'm afraid of Rupert. I wouldn't dare show him the book. He'd be far worse than you are."

"Worse than I am?" Lydia laughed. "I *am* sorry, Em. I have been harsh on your adventure, haven't I?"

"It's *not* an adventure! You keep dismissing me, dismissing any possibility that I could seriously believe what I'm telling you!"

Lydia looked away, ashamed to realize the truth in Emmeline's accusation.

"I'm sorry," Emmeline said, fighting with the tears that had started. "I should have known better. I'm sure I need to be going. I won't trouble you with this again. Please, let's forget I mentioned it."

"Emmeline, dear. Dear, dear Emmeline, I've upset you. I haven't helped at all. I'm sorry."

"No. It's all right. I can see I shouldn't have brought it up. I really must get back home. Please forget what I . . ."

"Don't go, Em. We can talk some more, and I'll listen and not criticize. Please sit down, dear."

"No. No, I'll be fine. But I can't stay. Thank you." She was gathering her skirts and moving toward the door, struggling to keep her tears in check.

"Emmeline, please forgive my shortness with you. You took me by surprise, you know. I'll listen . . ."

"Not now, Lydia. I'm going now. Later." She hurried out of the parlor and let herself out the front door. Lydia followed but did not try further persuasion, and Emmeline was gone.

Four

Henry Glendrake's family were known and respected as yeoman farmers who had tilled the land and adjoining acreage near Horse Stone House for over two centuries. His father also plied the trade of wheelwright, which Henry naturally learned, though he preferred working the land and husbanding livestock. As a boy, he had applied himself with uncharacteristic zeal to learning in the parochial school where he caught the attention of the vicar, Reverend Anthony Preese, who saw in him an unusually studious dedication and ready intelligence. The boy dressed well, was clean in his personal habits, and was perhaps even a bit fussy. The vicar took particular interest in his assiduous student, spending time with him almost daily.

The vicar was the bastard son of Sir Oswald Preese Graddell, a wealthy baron, whose allegiance to tradition allowed no inheritance for his illegitimate offspring, yet as the boy grew, the baron softened a little and came to recognize him officially, blessing him with the dubious privilege of carrying his name. He also saw to the boy's education, noting that his propensities were strongly religious, and he eventually offered his influence to obtain a vicarage for him, an offer young Anthony refused. Always conscious of the opprobrium of his unsanctioned birth, Anthony gradually distanced himself from his father and obtained a vicarage on his own merits and ingenuity, for his intelligence and particular brilliance with language and his flair for the classics were sufficient to win favor and recommendations from his dean and his dons, and ultimately gain the attention of Sir Rodney Farnsworth Braden, a long-time friend of the dean. Anthony did not mind that he had settled for a lesser situation than his father's influence might have won for him. He preferred the relative isolation of his rural assignment and the friendship that developed between him and Sir Rodney, as well as the satisfaction of having achieved it alone, but he never lost the awareness of the social irony that tolerated and even excused his aristocratic father's intellectual and moral shortcomings while essaying to limit the possibilities available to his bastard child. The nation's social structure often betrayed her most promising sons. Perhaps Anthony saw a little of himself in young Henry Glendrake, on whom nature had lavished abundant gifts while society decreed his limitations, just as he, Anthony Preese, had surpassed his now-dead father's accomplishments and those of his legitimate siblings who languished in relative uselessness while living on their inheritance. Perhaps Anthony pondered the delectable possibility that he could provide proper education and coaching for a boy who might transcend society's smothering lack of expectation and miserly foresight. Whatever his motives, Reverend Preese seemed determined to see Henry progress as far as his inclinations might take him, making suggestions to refine his diction and shape his articulation. At length, he drew Sir Rodney into his scheme to extend the boy's advantages.

Sir Rodney Farnsworth Braden, known simply as Squire Farnsworth to the vicar's parishioners, practiced careful philanthropic service designed to mold promising and deserving youth into solid contributing citizens, and he frequently, on the vicar's recommendation, would sponsor extended opportunities for education in London or Liverpool. The squire visited the vicar's school often, observing the teachers the vicar engaged, studying their methods, ever ready to make recommendations and suggest improvements. He took occasion to observe Henry Glendrake, both during recitations and in private interviews. Such interviews were conducted frequently by the squire or his spouse, as part of their active involvement in the youngsters' development. His impressions of Henry were decidedly favorable, and he agreed with the vicar to fund the boy's progress, but it was at that time that Robert, Henry's father, met with an unusual carriage accident and lost his life. Henry suddenly became the title-holder and inheritor of Horse Stone House and its small but fertile acreage. Loathe to abandon his studies, he continued with the vicar whenever possible, but his new responsibilities absorbed most of his time, especially when his mother's health began to wane, requiring even more of Henry. He found himself particularly pressed in the matter of his marriageable sisters, the most urgent concern of his ailing mother. He consulted with Reverend Preese, with whom by now he was comfortably familiar while keeping the respectful distance demanded by manners and tradition. Reverend Preese steered him toward several eligible candidates and even urged them along when they showed interest, and slowly the vicar, Henry, and Henry's mother managed to see two of the three girls married to men of integrity and reasonable substance. Then the fickleness of fortune altered the scene with a suddenness that left Henry reeling. His mother succumbed to her nagging illness, and within two weeks of her death, Reverend Preese, walking leisurely one afternoon in Squire Farnsworth's garden, stopped abruptly, clutched his chest, released a short gasp, and fell, striking his head and peeling the left side of his face in the gravel of the garden path. Quite without warning, his heart had stopped.

Henry bore the shock with characteristic stoicism but put off the project to find a suitable husband for Temperance, his sister, younger by six years. Squire Farnsworth, also shaken by the vicar's precipitous passing and feeling the urgency to see that the community was provided with a replacement as quickly as possible, conferred immediately with the bishop of the diocese and also with the old friend who had been Reverend Preese's sponsor, the dean of the college of theology at Cambridge. Hugh Morecroft, a promising young bachelor and a very recent graduate, was the dean's recommendation.

A quick review of Morecroft's qualifications impressed the bishop, but he held some reservation concerning the young man's background. He was the son of a tradesman. The bishop demurred for several weeks, explaining to Squire Farnsworth that ideally a man of the cloth should be in a position of influence with gentry as well as yeomen and commoners. A tradesman's son might win the respect of the lower classes but could hardly hope to command more than mere sufferance among those of higher standing.

Squire Farnsworth snorted.

"We've been over two months without our vicar, who, I remind you, sir, was the bastard son of one of our 'higher born' citizens. Seems a bit far-fetched, doesn't it, that an educated tradesman's son and a man of integrity is not fit to show us the way to follow a lowly carpenter, what?"

The bishop seemed not to need further deliberation. Young Hugh Morecroft moved into the vicarage with the bishop's blessing, however reluctantly bestowed.

Reverend Morecroft, breathlessly eager to earn his place in the community and provide the spiritual leadership so efficiently exemplified in his much more mature and highly respected predecessor, scurried about visiting parishioners and consulting with Squire Farnsworth, whose qualifications as an advisor could scarcely be impugned, to discover how he might prove his capability and devotion to his office, which he sincerely regarded as sacred. Squire Farnsworth obliged readily, generously helping the new vicar make connections of value, explaining needs and expectations. He made a particular point of mentioning Henry Glendrake, who had recently suffered the loss of his mother, and Henry's young sister, Temperance, who was still deeply affected and grieving. Reverend Morecroft responded at once, pleased to make the acquaintance of faithful parishioners who needed his assistance.

His arduous efforts to brighten Temperance's spirits and persuade her back to cheeriness (which, everyone told him, was her native disposition) had results far more extensive. His visits eventually brought smiles and laughter and awakened a volubility he found most attractive. Discovering that his original mission was accomplished, he then found that he had no inclination to suspend or even attenuate his visits to Horse Stone House. He enjoyed Henry's company; in fact, Henry became his friend, a very worthy friend.

But Henry was not the real motive for his lingering interest. He simply could no longer do without Temperance's eager glances, her dimpled smile, and contagious laughter. He solemnly and with perfectly correct formality asked Henry, Temperance's guardian, for his sister's hand. Henry demurred only long enough to consult with Temperance, and finding her eagerly agreeable, gave his consent.

All of Henry's sisters were now properly and comfortably wed. His mother could rest in peace.

Five

Squire Farnsworth was genuinely disappointed that Reverend Preese's plans for Henry could not materialize, but his favorable impressions did Henry no harm, as the squire used him to service his carriages when new wheels were needed or old ones needed repair. He trusted his skill with livestock as well and often required his herdsmen to follow Henry's advice in questions of their husbandry. Such confidence did not escape notice elsewhere in the community, and the wedding of Temperance to Hugh Morecroft added to Henry's distinction.

Henry did not seem to notice and probably never knew how much his prosperity was enhanced by Reverend Preese's high opinion of his erstwhile pupil or by the squire's good graces and lavish praise of his abilities. As for Hugh Morecroft, Henry never saw him as a step toward greater repute but only as his sister's husband, a man he had grown very fond of, notwithstanding his rather affected style as a preacher. Henry simply went about his business, tending his livestock and tilling his ground with zealous care, aware of the vicar's kindly regard for him, of course, and the squire's friendly disposition. But he did prosper. When necessary, he could hire itinerant help to harvest crops. He had a full-time stable hand, several journeyman wheelwrights, and apprentices. His father before him, quite frugally, had only two domestic servants, a cook, and a maid. Henry never saw a need to change that arrangement. Years passed. Henry was now over thirty.

His responsibilities as yeoman master of Horse Stone House did not render him oblivious to his own singularity, but they did limit his ability to pursue a remedy. He had seen one girl at a discreet distance, had perhaps spoken to her in the most superficial of circumstances, but did not really have the privilege of her acquaintance. He knew her name. Lydia. She was no doubt beyond him anyway, but he had not failed to notice her—the youngest of Squire Edward Smirthwaite's daughters. She was comely, with a slender waist, splendid brown eyes that seemed both warm and challenging, and dark brown hair neatly bunched at the back with loose curls about her face; her nose was just a bit too prominent to allow her to claim perfect proportion for her face, yet the package was most pleasing, and he wished fervently that she were more accessible.

He could not know, of course, that she was the cause of considerable frustration to her mother, who despaired of ridding her household of this last burden. All Lydia's sisters had married advantageously. The girl had a troublesome, tactless habit of speaking her mind and saw no particular advantage to her privileged birth, and no imposition of authority or persuasion, however firm or however mild, made any difference. She teetered forever on the edge of impropriety, a perpetual embarrassment. Unfortunately, her father's permissiveness gave the girl no proper encouragement. And added to her irksome tendencies, she was sickly. It was known that her lungs had suffered some kind of damage, or perhaps it was a birth defect, but attacks could be expected from time to time, and a knowledge of such a weakness was certainly no advantage in getting her properly placed. And even more exasperating was her indifference: She had, in spite of all her drawbacks, dismissed or put to flight a half-dozen suitors.

Lydia's father, on the other hand, doted on her. Having no male heir, he delighted in her company, quite openly preferring it to that of any of the other girls. She could be relied upon to challenge the validity of a male-dominated, male-structured society, and she sided in principle with the suffrage movement. She had been instructed as befitted her station and chafed at the fact that women could not expect the breadth of opportunities available to men, who carried the responsibility of livelihood and honor and were expected to exercise enlightened and benevolent leadership, with the right to vote. She argued that women's responsibilities required as much preparation as men's and doubted that men as a whole voted any more intelligently than women would had they the franchise. Her father found her independent and vigorously defended views both admirable and amusing, probably not expecting that his liberality would be taxed shortly.

When Squire Smirthwaite needed wheel repair, Squire Farnsworth named Henry Glendrake as the man most qualified, and Squire Smirthwaite did not hesitate to engage him. Henry did not consider sending one of his journeymen; he was quite sure he could manage this job better than the best alternative. Lydia's face haunted his daydreams as he began work in Squire Smirthwaite's well-equipped blacksmith shop. Under pressure to speak only the truth, the squire himself would probably have confessed that he noticed his favorite daughter's sudden and quite intense interest in the process of wheel replacement and repair as the project unfolded in his carriage house and blacksmith shop. It is not precisely known how Henry and Lydia found it possible to spend enough time in each other's company to fall in love, but the verifiable fact is undisputable. Henry, all too aware of the differences in their circumstances, demurred when it came time to speak with Lydia's father, but Lydia, with the boldness of indomitable independence and her confidence in her father's affection, cleared Henry's path by explaining to her father with unabashed candor that she had found the man she wanted to marry, and would he please be ever as kind, loving, and generous as she had always known him to be, and help her, please, to convince her mother and make it easy for Henry to ask for her hand, please, Father, please?

Squire Smirthwaite did not acquiesce immediately, though he truly liked Henry, who had earned praise from both the old vicar and Squire Farnsworth and now was the brother-in-law of the new vicar. Besides, he had heard quite enough complaints from his fretting consort that their daughter had no doubt managed to frighten off the last of her eligible suitors, and Henry was prosperous and respected, though not of high birth. And he could see that Lydia loved him. Typically, she did not regard the consequences of their inequality a serious matter. She would accept those consequences for the company of a man who not only tolerated but welcomed her forthrightness and loved her as honestly as she loved him, which among her criteria was far more important than a title. Perhaps she was right. The squire smiled to himself. Perhaps it would do his headstrong daughter good to discover whether her liberal theories could stand the test. She would spurn suitors with connections and marry a tradesman farmer decidedly beneath herself, just for affection and compatibility. Even if the arrangement lacked all the blessings of society, perhaps in the long run the bargain was not unfavorable. He would give *his* blessing, even if his society might not be so generous. If anyone could survive the challenge, Lydia could.

Mrs. Smirthwaite reacted just as expected but calmed down after the good squire's gentle, firm reminder that she had spent a great deal of energy convincing anyone who would listen that Lydia had already exhausted her chances for a proper alliance through her incorrigible tactlessness and scandalously liberal views. She subsided at last, if not totally won over, at least reconciled by Henry's congeniality and the generally favorable endorsement he had won among respected citizenry, including many of the gentry.

Lydia sank back into the chair she had drawn close to the fire. She slowly wagged her head, stared at the flame's hypnotic dance, and shook her head again, baffled by Emmeline's passionate reaction. She had hurt her friend; with the best of intentions she had tried to dismiss the matter as unimportant. Emmeline had always been so malleable, so docile, so willing to accept Lydia's judgment, but her response today . . . No, this was not a passing curiosity, a fad of only momentary persistence. Something had affected her friend far more deeply than she imagined. And she feared it. Yes, she herself had felt an aversion, a . . . fear? Was she afraid? Emmeline's request was simple, a plea for help. *Please read the book and tell me if I'm wrong.* And Lydia told her she was wrong without ever knowing what had affected her because . . . Well, there are a few things one knows without having to suffer the proof through actual experience. She knew that she could not live underwater just because fish managed it. One can know a few things quite instinctively, and she knew God didn't abandon His divine majesty and come down to consort with human beings.

Emmeline had used the argument that He had done so in the past. He had even come through the mortal experience and suffered crucifixion.

True enough, but the real proof lay in the historic reality that He hadn't done so in many centuries—since the advent of the Bible.

But Emmeline's question was simply, "Why not?"

Surely, it's a matter of faith. One has faith in the Bible, and in the vicar's word, and . . .

Why not?

―――

Henry entered his house after a cold day in his barn where he tended his cattle and plied his trade as a wheelwright. He smiled. Lydia was close to the fire, reading to the two children, Helen, five and a half, and Forest, three. Helen sat absorbed in the reading while Forest's attention wavered. Seeing his father, Forest sprang from his mother's lap to leap into Henry's embrace. Helen's slower response registered both her pleasure and vexation. She loved to welcome her father but hated any interruption in her mother's narrative. With Forest still clinging to him, Henry sidled toward the fireplace and its glowing summons and bent to kiss the top of Lydia's head. He next bent and blew his breath against Helen's neck, making her wince and squeal with delight.

"That tickles!" she protested.

Henry nodded to Lydia to continue reading. Helen, obviously gratified, snuggled closer to her mother. The reading ritual was soon over, and supper followed. The children were as noisy as ever, but Henry noticed a distance, an unusual quiescence in Lydia's demeanor, and when the children were finally bedded down, he drew her to him, hugged her wordlessly before whispering, "Ye're a long way away, lass."

"What?" Unconsciously defensive, she pulled away from him.

"Ah, I know you of old, woman. Too many years to be fooled. When you're quiet, it's because something has jolted you. Did I forget something I should have done?"

Lydia smiled. When he teased, he often used less-than-polished diction and even resorted to the slang. Then she became "lass." She knew he could speak as well as any gentleman around, including her own father, but often, when relaxed at home, he spoke in the yeoman dialect of his childhood. She actually loved his chiding about her loquacity. Teasing with Henry was always affectionate.

"So I'm too quiet for you, then?"

"You read to the children and haven't spoken since except when it couldn't be avoided. Are you ailing, then?"

"No, nothing ails me."

"No coughing, wheezing?" Her lung weakness was a persistent worry.

"No, none of that. I'm fine."

"That relieves me some, but not all. Hm?"

"I can't tell you, Henry. It wouldn't be . . ." She remembered Emmeline's words: "It's not seemly to hide things from your husband, is it?" She finished, ". . . wouldn't be seemly."

"Confiding in your husband unseemly?"

He was doing his best to appear shocked, and she loved him the more as she saw the spark of laughter lurking, stalking her behind his serious expression. Was that why she loved him? Well, it was one of the reasons. She smiled at him.

"You know I'll finally tell you, don't you?"

"Tell me? So you are hiding something from me. I'm shocked, my dear. I must see to your punishment in due order. Shall we go to bed?"

"It won't go away, I'm afraid." She laughed. "I suppose there is some irony in this, isn't there?"

"I'm quite baffled, my dear. Since I have no clue . . ."

"I mean, my having something I have to keep secret and your dying of curiosity because you always say I can never keep secrets and always speak my mind."

"Dying of curiosity, then? Hm. Good night, my dear," he said, leaving her standing as he walked to the bedroom. She followed.

"Henry . . . I do need you. I need your help, I think. I'm sure. I've hurt Emmeline's feelings . . ."

"Emmeline, is it? What have you two been plotting? Ah, no, you mustn't tell me, of course. I don't want to know."

"Oh, Henry, you know I can hide things from my mother, my father, my siblings, my friends—and even from you, if I've a mind."

"Well, have you?"

"Have I what?"

"Have you a mind?"

"I'll ignore the insult in that question. I've not a mind to tell you."

"Then I suppose I can't rescue poor Emmeline, can I, since I don't know what I'm rescuing her from."

"Maybe I would tell you, if you could drop that silly superior air and stop pretending I'm dying to let you in on it."

"Hm. Good night, my dear."

The game was too obvious. She knew she should counter by offering her own sweet "good night," following him silently to bed and letting him stew until morning. Or perhaps forever. She said nothing and excused herself to get ready for the night. When she joined him, he looked comfortably indifferent in the bed. They did their ritual devotions: he held the Bible close to the candle and read from one of the gospels, reached the end of the passage, and blew out the flame.

"Henry?"

"Mmm. Yes, my dear."

"I'm worried. Really worried. I would like your help."

"Um. If I can. What is the matter? If I may know that, now . . ."

"I promised Emmeline I wouldn't say anything, and I won't . . ."

"Well, then . . ."

". . . to anyone but you. She could be in very great trouble at home if any of this should reach Mr. Plowhurst."

"Rupert's involved, then? He's a bit of a bully, but . . . What's she done that might set him off?"

"She's seeing a preacher."

"Good heavens! She's . . ."

"No, not romantically. He's preaching his religion to her. Says he has a new church."

"A new one? Why the devil would anyone want a new one? We haven't got anywhere in particular with the old ones, have we? What is he? Not Catholic, not Church of England. Is he Methodist?"

"No, I don't think so. He's a missionary from America. Says some prophet over there talked with God and then wrote a book about it. Emmeline has the book and believes it. She hides it under her mattress. Can't afford to let Mr. Plowhurst find out, of course."

"No. Would cause a bit of a pucker, wouldn't it?"

Lydia said nothing. The room was quiet. Then: "She wants me to read it."

"What?"

"The book. She wants me to read it."

"Good heavens, whatever for?"

"Says she believes it and wants me to see why, I expect."

"Wants a convert, then? Great millstones, Lydia, she's lost her reason."

"I don't think so, Henry. She seemed sane as ever. Just perplexed and suffering."

"Suffering?"

"She's very affected by all this. Seems genuinely concerned about the book and what it contains."

"You didn't promise to read it, did you?"

"No. In fact, I rejected her outright, and that's what troubles me. She asked for my help, didn't she? Asked me to help her, and I refused. Not what friends do for each other, is it?"

"Well, you did the proper thing, no question about that. A few things people may expect of their friends, but studying blasphemous writing isn't one of them. She'll no doubt see her folly in a week or two and come asking your pardon for an absurd request."

"Yes, that's about what I told her. Then she said something that reminded me of you, something that you would say in the same circumstance, Henry. She said, 'I have read a book that you haven't read. Can you judge it better than I?' Those aren't her exact words, of course, but that was the question. Wouldn't you have said something like that?"

"Um. Perhaps. Well, yes, I suppose I would. But I don't go about reading religious nonsense, do I?"

"But don't you see? You're doing just what I did. Judging without substance."

"Without substance? Some fanatic in America says he hob-nobs with God, and that's substance? I don't have to read a book if I know beforehand that it concerns a sincere belief that the moon is made of cheese. Some books aren't worth the bother it would be to read them at all. If you know beforehand, why torture yourself with it?"

"But friendship . . . Isn't that worth a little bother? I love Emmeline. I *value* her. Would I injure myself—or you—if I did what she asks?"

"No, of course not. But it would be a miserable experience, and then what? Then you'd have to face Emmeline with the fact that she's making herself look foolish, and you'd have to tell her so."

"I already did. And that's when she pointed out that I really was judging her without a proper knowledge of her problem. Because it's a book that talks about God, and I can't help thinking our Bible does that—the very Bible you just read to me a few minutes ago."

"Now don't be makin' that kind of comparison. That *is* blasphemous, isn't it?"

"And our Lord was once called a blasphemer, wasn't He, when He said outright that He was the Son of God. Can't we jump too quickly to condemn, Henry? That's exactly what I did this afternoon. I have no thought, not even the shade of a thought, that I'll find anything commendable in the book; I'll probably hate it abominably, but shouldn't I help my friend?"

"I wouldn't read the fool thing for all the gold in the isle where I'm standin', but you do what you please. I'll say no more."

"You're not standing, you're in bed, and I wouldn't do it for gold, either! I'd do it to help Emmeline."

"Then do it, lass. But I want no part of it. I'm glad she didn't ask me."

Lydia smiled in the darkness. "That would have been something! Emmeline coming to you with her intimate secrets!"

"Why not? I'm trustworthy. I'd have kept it to myself, just as she asked."

Lydia struck him a blow on the arm with her fist. "You *know* I had to tell you! I'll never hear the end of it, will I?"

"Probably not. Good night, my love."

Six

Rupert Plowhurst nursed a keen consciousness of his social superiority, or what he could claim of it, in reality or imagination. He knew Henry, had known him from infancy, shared time with him in the parochial school and held grudging respect for his intelligence and resented the favor he had won from both the vicar and Squire Farnsworth. Plowhurst's inheritance did not include a title, though his mother was a product of minor nobility who married beneath herself in desperation as a withering spinster. Through her connections, Rupert's father had been able to increase his modest holdings and acquire some prestige in the community of farmers. Mrs. Plowhurst's air of superiority alienated most of her neighbors, and though her husband never forgot his own less pretentious beginnings, their son seemed predisposed to favor his mother's haughty selectivity. He grew up with supercilious preferences, but as he reached the season of marriageability, he found himself, as his mother had before him, rejected on several occasions, and his father felt obliged to intervene. Farmer Howard Hamilton had a daughter, not surpassingly comely but of age and possessing a certain quiet charm. Farmer Hamilton owed Mr. Plowhurst a modest amount of money but found himself unable to repay it. Mr. Plowhurst quietly negotiated with Farmer Hamilton, agreeing to cancel the debt in exchange for Farmer Hamilton's cooperation in securing a bride for Rupert.

Emmeline's temperate disposition made her easy to entreat, and though at first she tried to plead with her father, his stone-faced intransigence persuaded her to try to see the good in her situation, and she even managed to grace the wedding ceremony with a wan but sincere smile and an incipient excitement in becoming a franchised member of society.

The excitement faded quickly, as Emmeline's expectations of congenial, tractable, and communicative relations with her husband were summarily dashed within the first weeks of the wedding. Amiable company was largely denied her. Only her mother and sister provided respite from her loneliness. And Lydia, Emmeline's childhood friend who by now had married Henry, lived near, very near. When Emmeline approached her dour-faced husband for permission to make a social call on Mrs. Glendrake, he did not refuse her immediately but did not consent either. Pondering the matter, he remembered that Lydia was Squire Smirthwaite's daughter, and the connection could possibly prove useful. After several days of brooding, he gave his grudging consent.

～⁓⁓⁓

Lydia lost no time in following up on her intention to square matters with Emmeline. As quickly as she could, she covered domestic expectations the morning after her conversation with Henry and then took a brisk, but not too brisk (she had to protect her weak lungs, and it was winter) walk toward the Plowhurst estate. She arrived in good order, silently praying that she wouldn't have to deal with Mr. Plowhurst, who was always cordial enough to her and quite respected Henry, but he was so insufferably self-important. How in the world did sweet Emmeline ever consent to spend her life with him? Bowed to pressure, of course. Emmeline was not independent enough to stand up to her father and refuse to marry his choice of her suitors. Her father apparently could see only that Rupert Plowhurst owned a sizable farm, managed it well, and held some prestige mingled with ridicule. All the prestige in the world could not justify the man's own exalted opinion of himself. Lydia's opinion of him, had he suspected it, would have shocked him.

Emmeline's footman met her at the door, just as Lydia's maid had met Emmeline the day before. The Plowhursts had a larger domestic staff than the Glendrake household could afford. Lydia had only her cook, a good one, and she had her Madge, dear little Madge, who loved the Glendrakes and helped with child tending, cooking, in fact all household chores, and practically anything that was asked of her. Mr. Plowhurst had several hired hands and allowed Emmeline a house maid who helped with the children, a parlor maid, a cook, and a footman. The footman invited her in, where Emmeline received her warmly, as always, but with a reservation in her manner that had never been there before.

"Would you have time to sit a while, Lydia?" Emmeline asked politely. Lydia felt the chill.

"Yes, please. The walk has taken my breath. These lungs of mine . . . Now, Emmeline, let me come to the point." She sighed as she sank into the comfort of Emmeline's parlor. "I'm afraid I couldn't forget, Em. Couldn't stop thinking about . . ."

"I'm quite prepared never to speak of it again, Lydia."

"Yes, you said so yesterday. And if we left it that way, it would stand between us forever, and that's not the way I want to be friends. Not at a distance, not with a suspicion that you hold offence that I might question your judgment. I can't leave you struggling against resentment. And I can't abide my own conscience flailing me because I refused to help you. And you really didn't ask much, did you?"

Emmeline answered slowly. "More than I should have, I suppose. I wonder what I would have done if *you* had asked *me*. I wouldn't have dared, would I? But Henry isn't quite as . . . um . . ."

"No, Henry spoils me, bless him. Now, where is it?"

"What?"

"The book, of course."

"Oh, you don't have to read it, Lydia. I know now I shouldn't have asked, and I'm quite adjusted to . . ."

"Forgive me if I don't believe you, dear. But remember, if I don't like what I read, I'll tell you so. That's the risk you're running."

Emmeline smiled broadly. "I'll run it gladly! Sit here. I'll be back directly." She giggled. "You know where I have to keep it. Isn't it wonderful that men never have to worry about changing the bed clothes?" She disappeared and returned almost at once with a small volume in black binding.

They chatted together for another hour, Emmeline clearly relieved and pleased, with an almost childish exuberance replacing the stiffness of her earlier manner. Lydia, on the other hand, held strong reservations. What would be Emmeline's reaction when she told her how foolish the book really was? How could she shatter that naive anticipation with the starkness of her negative assessment? Because there could be no other option: She would have to destroy Emmeline's illusions and perhaps injure a cherished friendship. She struggled to remain cheerful, although the dread of that future moment weighed on her thoughts. Finally, she made an urgent plea that she must return home, and Emmeline reluctantly consented to her taking leave. Lydia wrapped her shawl about her and put on her cloak. Both were startled when Rupert Plowhurst walked in. Emmeline's cheeks colored, but she managed to smile broadly. "Rupert! You surprised me. I thought you told me you would be in Eccleston today."

"I changed my plans. My business in Eccleston is not pressing, and it will be more convenient to combine a couple of errands, the one I planned for today and my need to speak with Squire Darrow next week. I can manage both next week. Hm. Pleased to see you, Mrs. Glendrake."

"Thank you, Mr. Plowhurst. I dropped in quite unexpectedly. Emmeline and I never seem to have enough time in each other's company. Nothing can quite take the place of a good friend's company, wouldn't you say?"

"Perhaps, if the friend doesn't waste my time with trivialities."

"Oh, we manage to cover a few of those, too," Lydia answered. The book in her hand, though not voluminous, felt heavy and conspicuous. She held it casually at her side, under her cloak, hoping he would not notice. "But among all the trivia, there is laughter and affection, and we also speak of things not the least trivial. Good friends can do that, can't they? Well, I'm delighted I got to see you, if only for an instant. I was on my way out, as you might have gathered." Smiling amicably, she nodded to Plowhurst, stretched her free hand to grasp Emmeline's for a quick squeeze, and walked calmly and resolutely out the gate, with a long breath of relief that Plowhurst had made no inquiry about the book she was carrying.

At supper that evening, she laid the book next to her plate, certain that Henry would note its presence, and her expectation was fulfilled with predictable results: Henry eyed the book and raised reproachful eyes to hers without a word.

"Thought you'd probably view it that way," Lydia said mournfully.

"Haven't said a word, have I?"

"Yes, you have. Your eyes talk, and just now they were eloquent."

"You have the blasted book, then. I can hardly dance a jig over it, can I?"

"No, Henry. But thanks for just grumbling a little and not making a row. I have to do this."

"Have to? *Have* to? Who's forcing you?"

"Not who, *what*. Friendship, Henry. Emmeline's friendship. I hurt her when I refused her, and it's not worth it. I read perfectly well, and I won't be injured greatly by examining it, will I?"

"Suppose not."

"Thank you, my old dear Henry. You love me anyway, don't you?"

"Now don't be makin' a sentimental pudding out of this. I wouldn't read that trash . . ."

"I know. 'For all the gold in the isle where you're standin'.' And you're still not standing, you're sitting. I'll keep you abreast of all the spicy stuff and satisfy your curiosity while I spare your sensibilities."

Lydia could not keep her promise to fill Henry in on her progress. When she began her reading, her loquacity seemed to disappear. She made no mention of the book at all, and Henry suffered some perplexity, although he refused to be drawn into any show of curiosity. Then a deeper concern crowded the matter to the periphery of his priorities. Lydia began coughing, occasionally wheezing, the frequent symptoms of relapse. Her lung ailment, again. He urged her to rest, and she ultimately acquiesced, as the coughing grew worse and her breathing suffered progressively. Henry took the two children the eleven-and-a-half miles to Lydia's sister, Catherine, left them there, and summoned Dr. Driscoll, the physician who always attended Lydia and knew her condition quite thoroughly. The doctor prescribed continued bed rest, a chest poultice, and a foul-tasting syrup prepared by the apothecary.

Emmeline dropped in as soon as she got word of Lydia's condition. Henry's concern had kept him close to Lydia's bedside to the detriment of his wheelwright business. Emmeline's assurance that she had secured Mr. Plowhurst's grudging permission to spend the afternoon attending Lydia persuaded Henry to leave things in her hands momentarily and spend a couple of hours catching up on work now in arrears. When he returned to the house, he entered quietly, hoping not to disturb his wife should she be sleeping. She was obviously awake; he could hear her chatting with Emmeline. He sat quietly in his chair near the fireplace and lit his pipe. The voices were faint, but there were no competing noises in the house, and he could distinguish their discourse quite clearly. Lydia's voice reached him first:

"I was surprised, of course. I expected your prophet to rhapsodize over his heavenly visions and dwell on all the reasons why the world should pay respect and homage to his great spirituality. It's not about that at all!"

"No."

"It's a . . . Well, what is it?"

"A history. Like the Bible."

"I suppose that's what surprised me. I found myself reading about a family that lived in Jerusalem a long time before the

Lord was born. I hadn't bothered to read the explanations at the beginning. You know, the stuff that tells how the man got it. What's his name?"

"Joseph Smith."

"Yes. Him. How he came by the record. But it isn't about Joseph Smith. It's that family that left Jerusalem and went to the Americas someplace."

"But what do you think of it, Lydia?"

"I don't know. Can't say I believe any of it, but . . ."

"But you don't think I'm crazy or just hopelessly foolish do you? I mean . . ."

"No, Emmeline. I'm sorry I made you feel that way. If you're deceived, it's not mere gullibility that did it. I have to confess, the feeling I get as I read is quite compelling. Frightens me, actually."

"Me too. I kept wondering, what if it's true? And I didn't want to wonder. I wanted to know it was a lie. But I couldn't feel that way. Now I have to believe. I've read it. Clear to the end. Then I started over. I've read most of it twice, and some of it over and over."

"Well, I stopped for a day or two. Had to rest, you know. This misery that follows me—these lungs of mine . . ."

"Are you tired? I don't want to . . ."

"Oh, no. I'm actually feeling much stronger. I promise to let you know when I need to sleep again. It's good to have your company. I wanted someone to hear my frustration. Henry's a dear, dear man, but he doesn't want to hear me say I'm puzzled by what I have read. He wants to hear me condemn it—just as I did when you first told me about it."

"I know. I can't speak to Rupert about it either. I don't suppose I ever will."

"Oh, I'll certainly speak to Henry. Sometime. I couldn't live with a constant silence between us. Silence is too lonely. It's solitude, and I'm not solitary. Henry, bless him . . . Speaking of Henry . . . I think I smell tobacco smoke!"

"Hm. Yes, I do too!"

Henry's pipe had betrayed him. He coughed nervously. "Yes, my dear. I came in and sat before the fire and lit me pipe. Almost without bein' aware of it. The price I pay for my vice, what?"

"How long have you . . ."

"Long enough, my dear. Hard for me to swallow, that I'll grant you. I'm findin' it hard to believe what I hear."

"But . . ." Lydia began, and then changed her mind. "Henry, why don't you join us? Let's not shout our conversation from room to room."

"I . . . I think I must go. Oh, mercy, look at the time! I really must . . ." Emmeline sputtered.

Henry strode into the parlor. "Don't let my opinion of your reading pleasure trouble you, Mrs. Plowhurst. I can't help the views I hold of the books you choose, but it doesn't hinder your welcome in my house or my gratitude for your friendship and concern for my wife."

"Henry, all we are doing is discussing what we have read. Remember, *we* have read it; you haven't."

Henry smiled reluctantly. "Then I'll not express my judgment, though my opinion has not changed. Thank you again, Emmeline, for helping me look after my Lydia."

Emmeline felt the dismissal, but it was offered so gently she could not resent it.

"It's always my pleasure, Mr. Glendrake."

"Em, dear, thank you for keeping me company," Lydia said. "Don't worry about Henry. His displeasure won't last. He's no tyrant and makes no unfair judgments. Do you, Henry?"

"My judgment is always justified, Mrs. Glendrake, whenever I consider that I chose you and asked for your hand. Your acceptance and your father's consent show that you confirm it, don't they?"

"Thank you, Henry. Now don't be harsh on our reading until you have seen it yourself, and that will clinch your good wisdom. Good-bye, dear Emmeline. Please come back soon. We've much more to discuss."

After Emmeline left, Henry was unsmiling as he inquired after Lydia's condition.

"You seem to be feeling better," he ventured. "Emmeline's visit seems to agree with you. Stronger now, are you?"

"Yes, I think so. Breathing is still a little painful, but I do feel stronger."

Henry's thoughts still kept his smile at bay. "Very good. Well, I suppose I need to return to the barn. Work in arrears, you know."

"Sorry. I'm causing you all sorts of trouble, aren't I?"

"Not a bit of it. But I must get my work done. Emmeline gave me a couple of good hours, though. Nice of her."

"I imagine Mr. Plowhurst makes it uncomfortable for her when she comes to pay a visit. Now what I just said was outright stupid. I don't imagine any such thing. I know for a fact that it's so. She has managed a little independence, though, but if he ever caught her reading her precious book . . ."

"As I have not the same hold over my wife, she is quite free to read it whenever she pleases, is that it?"

Lydia rarely saw him irritable. "But . . . Henry, you gave me your permission. Something Rupert Plowhurst would never have the courtesy to do. And I'm grateful. Please don't turn contrary on me now. I'm not harmed by it, am I?"

"I'm not sure. You sounded almost—um—seemed quite receptive?"

"Receptive? To Emmeline? Of course!"

"I mean the blasted book. Either you've changed completely–afraid of hurting Emmeline's feelings–or you're actually reading the thing with some pleasure."

Lydia's face grew solemn. A slight flush crossed her features, changing momentarily the pallor her illness had stamped upon her. "It does surprise me. I suppose I am even a little relieved to be able to tell Em that I don't see her as a complete incompetent for finding it—compelling. I've never told her that I share her belief."

"I expected you to see its folly immediately. That you have not seen it yet is surprising to *me*."

"Well, don't get out of sorts over it. I'm reading it to give Em my honest opinion, and I have. I won't give her a dishonest report to spare her feelings, and I didn't expect you would want anything less when I report to you, would you?"

Henry straightened and drew in his breath. "Of course not. Of course not. Well, then, I still have work to do, don't I?" He strode out with an uncharacteristic stiffness.

~ ~ ~

Sunday morning, Henry came to breakfast dressed for Sunday services, protesting that Lydia, still pale and obviously not fully recovered, should remain in bed, but she followed him to the table, insisting that she was strong enough now and would no longer give in to her weakness. She did agree to stay home from services, and Henry insisted that Madge must remain with her, and she would have charge of the children as well. They would make services unbearable should he try to take them with him alone.

Madge did her best to look disappointed. She understood little of Sunday ritual but always followed dutifully to church, knowing it was expected and that she was needed to help with the children. She felt guilty without ever knowing why when the vicar, now part of the family, waxed forceful in his admonitions for greater goodness, or upbraided the congregation for its neglect or indifference toward whatever worthwhile project he was currently endorsing or sponsoring, projects that always lay beyond her understanding or her field of capability. She knew that Henry admired the vicar. She, on the other hand, saw him as aloof, cold, judgmental. Henry praised him for his involvement in all deserving aspects of communal activity and frequently commended his sermons. His views of the vicar's preaching style, however, did seem to harmonize with hers.

"I wish he had fewer airs," he grumbled one day.

"Heirs?" Lydia questioned. "What heirs? Temperance has given him but one, and he is not likely to inherit for another fifty years. Besides, Hugh will never command a fortune, nor would he be likely to name us as inheritors even if he did. And he'll probably outlive both of us, so why do you care how many heirs he has?"

Henry regarded her blankly and then brightened and laughed when her misapprehension dawned on him. Nothing dawned on

Madge. The conversations between her much-loved employers often left her quite bewildered.

"I mean the airs he puts on when he's at the pulpit. I wasn't referring to the other kind, the ones spelled with *h*," Henry explained.

Lydia shrugged and simply said, "Oh." Madge grasped only that Henry felt as she did about the vicar's high-toned sermons.

Henry did not take his carriage to church, as would have been necessary had the family been able to accompany him, but rode his mare and tethered her with other horses tended by a lad hired to see to their safety.

Hugh's sermon that morning was probably well-crafted and timely, but Henry could not tell. It was delivered in Hugh's stylized fashion, and Henry's thoughts hovered elsewhere. After services, he struggled between a desire to hurry home and the urge to talk with Hugh. Temperance hailed him just as he gave in to his homing impulse and had almost reached the door.

"Henry!" she called, breaking away from one of the parishioners who was gushing over her husband's "remarkable" sermon. "Excuse me, Mrs. Clyde, I must speak with my brother."

Henry waited at the door, smiling his affection at his youngest and liveliest sister.

"You're not leaving? I haven't had a chance to see you or speak with you in . . . how long? More than two weeks, at least. How is Lydia?"

"Better, I'm sure. Yes. Really much better. Otherwise, I would have stayed home with her as I did last week, but she's not yet well enough to be up and about. Madge cares for her quite adequately, though, and Lydia herself encouraged me to come today, so you see . . ."

"Henry, so good to see you. How is Lydia?" The vicar himself interrupted, having disengaged himself from another obsequious parishioner.

"He was just telling me, Hugh. You interrupted him," Temperance complained.

"Sorry, my dear. Sorry, Henry. Rude of me, what?"

"Not at all, Hugh. I was just telling Temperance that Lydia's much improved. Enough so that I felt quite assured she could do without me while I attended your services. I should hurry home though."

"Can't you stop by the vicarage for a bite to eat? Wouldn't take but a minute, and I haven't seen you in an ice age," Temperance offered.

"No, probably not today, love. Lydia could conceivably miss me. I'm really quite indispensable to her, you know."

"No doubt, no doubt," Hugh spouted, taking Henry's hyperbole quite seriously.

Temperance tossed her head and rolled her eyes. "I'm sure you are, Henry," she said, blunting her voice with irony. "Well, I must hurry home as well, though I'm far from indispensable. Dinner does want my attention, however." She smiled at them both and skirted with sprightly step around another parishioner who was approaching her husband, and walked cheerfully away, bound for the vicarage.

Hugh mumbled his excuses to the encroaching parishioner and followed Henry as he walked briskly to where he had left his mare.

"Can we do anything for poor Lydia?" Hugh persisted.

"Not much one *can* do, Hugh. It's the old lung problem, you know. Dr. Driscoll keeps a wary eye on her. The condition comes and goes. She's improving, as I said earlier." A short silence preceded his change of thought: "What do you know of the itinerant preachers from America?"

"Preachers from America? Haven't heard. What are they preaching?"

"Apparently it's some new sect. They have a book. Supposed to be a revealed history of some sort. I haven't read it, of course, but Lydia had it thrust upon her just before she fell ill." Henry hesitated, watching Hugh's puzzled reaction. When he picked up his thought again, his voice had a pinched, dry quality. "She finds it interesting."

"You don't know the name of the sect?"

"No. Didn't bother to find out. Not much interested in that sort of thing. Seems some fellow in America had a chat with God and wrote it all down in this book, or some such nonsense."

"A chat with God? But . . . but that's pure blasphemy. Surely Lydia didn't . . ."

"No, I don't think so. She's not one to swallow without chewing. All she said was it was—um—compelling, I believe was her word for it. Yes, that was what she said. Compelling. I really can't say beyond that. I'm sure she'll wind up laughing at it all later. I was just curious; wondered what you could tell me."

"I'm afraid it's quite outside my familiarity. I trust Lydia's not—ah—her judgment's not affected by . . ."

"No, Hugh, she's not delusional. Just a passing curiosity, I expect. Nothing to be concerned over."

He mounted his mare and cast Hugh a rather rueful smile as he rode away.

Seven

Though the days that followed returned Lydia her strength and vitality, they also grew more perplexing. Henry had never responded boorishly to anything; not ever. Lately he seemed at great challenge to smile or react cheerily to any circumstance or give answer except in monosyllables, and that only under pressure. She tried to speak with him about it and he dismissed her curtly. He even seemed hard put to show his usual affection to his children. Tension hung heavily in the household. Henry scowled if Lydia went out, though his morose presence offered no recompense for remaining. Devotions at night became routine, habitual, devoid of any spiritual substance. Meals grew tedious. Steak and kidney pie, forever a favorite, inspired no compliment or gesture of pleasure; plum pudding brought no response. Cold cider nor sweet wine—nothing could elicit the praise the erstwhile Henry would have lavished readily.

Several days of this and Lydia knew it must not continue. Her life had always inspired criticism from the prim, the proper, the proud, and the ones she could never abide. Never mind that they returned the sentiment. Henry had been attracted to her precisely because she spoke her mind without euphemisms or circumlocutions. What was all this about, then? She was reading a book, a book with a simple title, *The Book of Mormon*, and she refused to treat it as he had expected. She found it interesting—well, not always; there were laborious moments, and some of it was downright difficult to swallow. But it was compelling and did not remotely suggest blasphemy, as she understood the concept. It was a Christian book, deeply, blatantly so. Emmeline had come to believe it totally, and Lydia had begun to see why. Henry could not accept any of this, and so he behaved with uncharacteristic rudeness. Where was the gentleness she married, the wholesome sense of fair play, the robust open-mindedness, the affectionate teasing?

If *he* had changed so drastically, she had not. It would have to be dealt with and not on the wordless terms he had offered–terms of arbitrary intransigence and stubborn silence.

She prepared for bed as usual and could see Henry waiting for her, his dour face against his pillow, the candle casting shadows over his features, making them even longer and more bitter.

"I won't bother with devotions tonight, Henry. They have lost all meaning of late anyway. I'll be sleeping in the parlor."

"What?"

"Oh, sorry. I didn't mean to wake you."

"I'm not sleeping. I'm as awake as you are. What the devil are you talking about?"

"I mean I got your attention, Henry dear. I'm not sharing the world you've thrust upon me. If you're going to continue behaving as if I had stolen your fortune and your honor, I shall move quietly out of your life, if that's what you want, and it seems that it is, so I'll start by moving out of your bedroom."

"What? You've taken complete leave of your senses, Mrs. Glendrake."

"If you're bent upon your own way without discussion or communication, I can spend my time with Catherine, and I'll take the children to keep them out of your way. Whatever it takes. Even going into service couldn't be much worse than what this house has become of late."

Henry was by now quite upright in his bed. "My dear, you're beside yourself. I can't imagine . . ."

"Don't strain yourself to pretend you don't know where this is coming from." She was crying now, her voice thickened by her tears, but they did not staunch the flow of her words. "You told me when we married how you admired my honesty and my inability to keep my opinion to myself. Admired it! Yes you did, Henry. Those were your words. 'I love you because you're not a mousy mop of a woman whose opinion merely reflects expectations.' That's what you said about me then. Maybe not exactly, but . . ."

"Of course. I've always admired that in you, Lydia."

"Then why this campaign to make me reverse myself and reflect only your opinion? I have read something I find . . . fascinating. And I can't even discuss it with you. You're offended because my opinion might not fit within your notion of propriety."

"Now, Lydia, you're not being fair. I'm not . . ."

"Fair? You're talking about fair? I know what I have read; you don't! You judged the book before you saw it, and it would be terribly uncomfortable to alter that judgment, wouldn't it? But it's fair for you to make a judgment about what I have seen and you haven't, and unfair of me to point out those little inconsistencies."

"Lydia, where is your . . . well, that plain common sense I know is you? You're not yourself at all . . ."

"And you are? That's what worries me. If the real Henry is the one I've lived with these last weeks, then the one I married got lost somewhere. And I want the other one, please."

Henry's voice tried to be conciliatory. "You're making too much of this, my dear . . ."

"The Henry I married gave his word. He said, 'Then do it, lass.' And I did. Now you're going back on it."

"I haven't uttered a word, not a word!"

"And words are all that can bind you, then? I'll grant, you haven't verbally reneged, but you've launched a tantrum, a tirade of silence, petulance, and moroseness. That's worse." She stomped to the door and then whirled and shrieked through her tears as she saw that Henry was stirring with the intent to follow her. "Don't you try to follow me, Henry. I'm not sharing my bed with you unless you chain me to it, and you'll need all your strength to do that, and the memory of it will be forever dear to me, won't it Henry? I'll be sure to thank you every day for your gentleness and understanding." She was weeping without control now, and she rushed out to find a place away from the bed she loved, the man she loved–loved, and at this instant, despised.

Henry sat stunned on the edge of his bed, the color draining from his face, panting as the scene in which he had been an unwilling player sank into his consciousness. He struggled with the anger that strove against his equanimity. He knew quite certainly that Lydia had meant what she said. Short of sheer force and brutality, nothing could persuade her to remain at his side. Of course he would not force her, chain her to him. Nagging at his conscience was the reluctant realization that she was right; he had given his consent for her to read that abominable piece of trash. He had not supposed at the time that she would actually do it. Later, after she had fetched the book from Emmeline, when his actions made it plain that he did not approve, he expected that she would acquiesce and put the thing aside. Now he was caught on the reality of his own misjudgment; he never should have consented. But he had, and had since behaved like a sulky child. As he sat there, drained of strength or the ability to make an intelligent move, the vision of Lydia's stricken, tear-streaked face as she accused him, shrieking out her indignation and hurt, taunted what was left of his tortured thoughts. And he knew above all else that he loved her. Faced with her threat, he blanched. Would she go so far as to leave him? Probably not, but spiritual distance is as cruel as physical distance; either way, she was not with him, and he cried inside himself, begged with her not to leave. But she was not at his side to hear his pleading.

Then a wave of greater despair washed over him. He had spoken with Rupert Plowhurst that very afternoon. The memory of the encounter did not reassure him.

Henry's business often obliged him to visit Eccleston township for supplies and contacts. Rupert Plowhurst, seeing him there, hailed him.

"Glendrake, a word with you, if you don't mind."

"Not at all, Rupert." Perhaps Henry sensed that such familiarity galled Rupert, but he never regarded this particular neighbor as any more highly born or highly placed than he and had always approached him as an equal. When tradesmen mistakenly addressed Rupert as "Squire Plowhurst, sir," he accepted the title as his due, whereas Henry, whenever anyone mistook him for what he was not, always proffered a mild protest, usually with a touch of humor, to correct the mistaken impression. Thanks to the vicar, he spoke with as much elegance as he wished, but he was not gentry, nor did he care for the distinction. He could speak much better than Rupert when he chose, though Rupert had endured his mother's petulant coaching all his life and would not think of lapsing into a yeoman's register, as Henry would often do at home with Lydia, perhaps teasingly, to remind her of the difference in their social positions and subtly to suggest that she had chosen him in spite of it.

"There's a pub just there, not a hundred yards from where we stand. Could you join me for a pint?" Henry invited.

Rupert nodded. They entered the shadowy pub, ordered their ale, and took it to a small table where they could expect some privacy. Henry said nothing, took a couple of healthy swallows from his tankard and then raised his eyes to meet Rupert's, but Rupert did not meet the inquiring gaze. He sipped his ale, cleared his throat, and then drew a breath, steeling himself for some unpleasantry, still looking away.

"What do you know of—ah—what is my wife . . . my wife and yours . . . what . . . ?"

"They seem to be very good friends, Rupert. They share good moments together, wouldn't you say?"

"I'm—ah—not at all sure that's what I would say, Glendrake. What else are they sharing?"

"It would seem to me that's information you should get from your wife. Certainly I'm not the one to give it to you, even if I have it." Henry knew he had blundered. "Even if I have it" suggested all too clearly that he *did* have it. He hurried on: "What I mean is, you and I, I expect, do not control our wives' views, and certainly not the friends they are entitled to keep company with. And *I* am not entitled to information she chooses to protect."

"No wife is entitled to views that oppose her husband's!" Rupert snorted. "You don't mean to tell me you permit that sort of thing? If we were to follow such a course it would do serious harm to a properly ordered society."

Henry cast his peevish companion a deprecating look, which Rupert could interpret any way he chose. "Your wife is up to no mischief, I'm sure. She and Lydia have come to exchange some views on religion and have also discussed readings from some book or other. Your wife got it from an itinerant preacher. No harm in it, I imagine. Not the sort of thing I'd waste my time with, of course . . ."

"Emmeline procured a book from an itinerant preacher? She failed to tell me . . ."

"Good heavens, man, give the poor girl the freedom of a little curiosity! What harm is there in reading a bit, if she finds it interesting?" *How strange,* Henry thought quite fleetingly. *I'm defending Emmeline, and I wish to thunder Lydia had never heard of the infernal book.* Was he being fair to Rupert to pass it off so lightly? Probably wouldn't matter. Rupert would take it too seriously even if it were a confirmed frivolity. "I wouldn't worry over it. Not worth the bother. Women have to amuse themselves, I suppose, and reading . . ."

"A useless waste of time, that's what it is! What business have they meddling in things they probably can't understand anyway? What's in the book they're reading? Some sort of novel, I suppose, but why would a preacher . . ."

"Couldn't say, of course. Haven't opened it. I'm neither interested nor concerned. Would suggest we just let the matter die."

―――※※※―――

The irony of his advice squeezed on his vitals like a cold vise. Just let the matter die, he had said—and he had precipitated the only serious rupture his marriage had ever suffered because he had *not* let the matter die.

How serious was it? What harm could come from it? It's sure to blow over with a little time, just as he suggested to Rupert. Silly to have behaved so churlishly, though. Silly to let trifles come between him and Lydia. He must find the way to apologize and make her know he meant it.

He slipped out of bed and made noiseless steps into the parlor where he expected to find her. His heart pounded harder than if he were facing mortal danger. He stopped, tried to control his breathing, which was so rapid he was sure it could reveal his approach. He hesitated, curiously fearful, and finally ventured:

"Lydia?"

No answer.

"Lydia? Please, love, I can't..."

"It won't do any good, Henry. I told you not to follow me."

"I couldn't help myself, love. I can't..."

"I'm afraid you have to! Now leave me alone!"

"Please, Lydia... Please don't turn me away. I'm trying to tell you..."

"You have nothing more to tell me! You've already judged me incapable of sound thinking. Do I have to leave this house to get some peace?"

"No. You don't have to leave. I want to say I'm sorry. Very sorry."

"Sorry for me? Because I'm so stupid as to read something you find offensive before you know what's in it? Am I so pathetic?"

"No. I'm the pathetic one. I'm sorry for behaving like a malevolent muckworm. I'm begging you to forgive me."

Lydia drew in a breath drenched in her tears. She held it and then let a tiny wail escape: "Oh, Henry...." She was weeping quite copiously now, and Henry sensed how desperately he was needed, and how he needed her. He hurried to her, folded her to himself, bursting with relief and remorse. She wept and clung to him.

"I'm sorry," she sobbed.

"No. You have nothing to be sorry for. You behaved with dignity and courage, and I... What if I had succeeded in changing you?

I would have spent my life loathing myself. Oh, Lydia, my Lydia, my cherished Lydia..."

She stopped him with a kiss, full of love and anguish and passion and relief. The moment held a tenderness never imagined, and his fingers caressed her face, her neck. Her breast heaved as she breathed and he kissed her. She shuddered and clung tightly. His lips traveled, languishing, lingering over her face, her neck, her shoulders...

Concern darkened Henry's disposition. Relieved on the one hand that tensions between him and Lydia had been resolved, on the other hand he felt quite at a loss. He never forbade her reading of "the book," the infamous book Emmeline had thrust upon her. What good could come of that? Lydia could not be coerced; she must be free or dead, and just as he had tried to reassure her, that independent spirit had attracted him, held him, fascinated him perhaps more than her slender waist, her disarming smile, and all the other physical attractions that adorned her. He would not change her for a throne or the gift of a universe. Men such as Rupert Plowhurst felt compelled to dominate, needed to sense power and superiority. Or, perhaps, to be fair, it was merely their need to defend and protect the weaker members of society. But what if that perception of inherent weakness were specious? With Lydia, Henry enjoyed a partnership, a true equality of intellect and judgment. He did not feel diminished, merely complemented, and could not see his wife as a helpless creature to be indulged; rather, hers was a superior mind that deserved parity with his or any other. How stupid, how utterly stupid, to yield to the notion that women were constitutionally of lesser stuff and by nature relegated to subservience. Yet he had nearly yielded to the prevailing view. But his relief that he and Lydia had reconciled did not acquit him from his perplexity where their differences were concerned. In all else, Lydia could see the reasonable side of things, pierce the veneer of sham with the cold acuteness of her mind. Why could she not see the absurdity, the consummate silliness of that American swain's claim, so obviously fatuous, that God had appeared and dictated a whole book to him?

He resolved simply to let time have its way with Lydia and her fascination with the Book of Mormon. Surely she would come to terms with reason and good sense, and any attempt at present to force the issue would bring negative results. He had already seen proof enough of that. Yet how could he quiet his own resentment against the perpetrators—whoever they were—of this unwholesome, unprincipled, probably even iniquitous movement that had so beguiled Emmeline?

When Lydia's health allowed it, she accompanied Henry and the children to church again. After services, they accepted Temperance's invitation to take tea at the vicarage. Henry half hoped, half feared, that their conversation might reach the topic of "the book." Hope and fear were both satisfied. Hugh suddenly broached the matter with a blunt question.

"I've been very curious about what you asked me a few weeks ago, Henry. Those itinerant preachers from America—I understand you've heard from them, Lydia?"

"No, I've only spoken with my friend Emmeline who has some sociability with a pair of missionaries, one of them American and the other English." She cocked her head slightly—her gesture of inquisitiveness. "Did Henry mention them to you?"

"Yes, I did," Henry answered a bit nervously before Hugh could lend the nuance of his interpretation to the situation. "Wanted to know what Hugh could tell me of them. Have you found out anything new, Hugh?"

"Not really. Only that Mrs. Plowhurst had incurred considerable displeasure from her husband for her interest in their preaching. I still cannot name their sect," he said, sipping at his tea.

"I don't know that either," Lydia confessed. "They gave Emmeline a very interesting book . . ."

"Oh, yes, Henry mentioned that, didn't you, Henry?"

"The Book of Mormon. Yes, I did mention it." There was a rueful note in his voice.

"You never gave me the title, though. *Book of Mormon?* Curious name, what?"

"Never heard of it," Temperance said, apparently feeling a bit marginated from their conversation.

"You might find it interesting, Hugh," Lydia suggested. "*I do.* I haven't finished it yet. I put it aside when I took to my bed, but I intend to finish it."

"What's it like?" Temperance asked.

"It's like reading the Bible," Lydia said simply.

Hugh raised his eyebrows; Temperance looked skeptical.

"Like reading the Bible? How peculiar. I've never read anything that could be compared to the Bible," Temperance suggested a bit defensively.

"You might try it," Lydia responded lightly. "It's quite a different story, but its . . . flavor . . . Is that the word I want? . . . is very like what I get when I read the Bible. Yes, as I think of it, that's how I must describe it. Does that answer your question?"

Temperance laughed. "I could hardly say, could I, since I have never laid eyes on it."

"You seem rather taken with it, Lydia," Hugh ventured cautiously, a touch of insinuation in his tone.

Lydia laughed. "You're just like Henry, Hugh. He couldn't abide my being drawn to it either. But what's the problem? How can I tell what's in it if I don't read it? And what harm, if what I read appeals to me?"

"It's the basic premise, Lydia, the preposterous assertion that God wrote it, or had something to do with the writing of it. One need go no further when the premise is an impossible one."

Henry smiled and said nothing. Let Hugh have the adventure Lydia could give him.

"Hugh," Lydia answered–as Henry knew she would. "Who wrote the Bible?"

Hugh seemed to see in her question no sequitur to his sweeping denunciation, or if he saw it, he felt so comfortably in his element that he could ignore it. "Various authors. The Pentateuch–the first five books of the Old Testament–was no doubt composed by Moses, but surely with help from other documents and possibly scribes and copyists. The rest, or most of the rest, give their names to the writing for which they are responsible. Scholars may haggle from time to time over the authenticity of some of the names, or whether it was really David who wrote the Psalms, or Solomon who composed most of Proverbs, but fundamentally, I see no purpose served in the haggling. Acts of the Apostles was written by a gentile convert, a physician, Luke, the same who writes the third of the Synoptic Gospels."

Lydia smiled submissively. "Then God is not the author of the Bible," she said softly.

Hugh answered with confidence, reassuringly, "Of course not directly, but His ways, frequently mysterious, are always inspired, and He is quite capable of getting His message to His foundering, struggling children, bringing about through imperfect but goodly servants His holy purposes. You must realize, though, the canon now is complete. His law has been given, and it is sufficient."

"Oh, I'm sure, Hugh. It's suddenly clear, and I'm relieved to know that we no longer need Him personally, since the Bible contains all He has to say to us, and the only servants worthy of speaking for Him are the dead ones we find in the Bible. You yourself are superfluous, aren't you, since you have nothing to add to the Bible that can enhance what's already been written."

The indignant surprise on Hugh's face as he tried to control his response brought a low chuckle from Henry, who found himself enjoying Hugh's failure to prove Lydia a mere petulant child who needed the guidance of superior reasoning.

"Do you mind if we get on with our tea?" Henry suggested lightly. "This discussion, unless we change it, promises to become unpleasant, what?"

"Of course, Henry," Lydia said, her voice sweetly modulated. "We must never discuss religion unless we agree never to disagree." She smiled. "Temperance, didn't you tell me that you were planning to rearrange the vicarage garden?"

Eight

Henry was sure Lydia had finished her book. He made no reference to it, nor did Lydia mention anything connected with it, but she did remark on Emmeline's curious silence. It had been days, weeks, since they had spoken.

"I'm concerned, Henry. I expected to hear from her long ago. Should I send a note to her? Madge could run it over."

"Sure it's wise?" Henry said softly.

"No. I can't be sure, can I? Something's amiss, though. Emmeline would keep in touch. I know she would. She was far too excited not to want . . . want to know . . ." She hesitated to finish.

Henry did not press, perhaps fearing what she might reveal of her own thoughts about Emmeline's religious convictions. After a short silence, Lydia continued, "I haven't seen her since you have, Henry. Not since we smelled you smoking your pipe."

"Not since then?"

"No. And you didn't frighten her all that much. Emmeline and I have survived much greater challenge than that. Actually, you were quite sweet in your forthright way, so I know you are not the problem."

"I hope not. Don't want the responsibility of any more mischief than I've already caused."

Lydia laughed. "Henry the mischief-maker! Dear, dear Henry, you did me no permanent harm. You surely have forgiven yourself by now." She wrapped her arms about him, and he smiled and nuzzled her neck gently.

"I spoke with Rupert the same day we . . . the night you left my bedroom in a huff. Did I tell you that? About Rupert, I mean."

"No, I don't think so. What about him?"

"You remember I went to Eccleston that day. Rupert hailed me, and we had a pint together. He wanted to know what you and Emmeline were up to. I assured him it was quite innocent." He saw her expression change. "I did, my dear. I even chided him a bit for not allowing his wife the freedom of a little curiosity. I thought I had convinced him."

"You told him about the book?"

"I mentioned that she had a book she obtained from an itinerant preacher, yes. Having accosted me, you know, demanding to know what I could tell him was going on between you and Emmeline . . . well, I told him what I could–that you had discussed some points of religion, all quite innocent, as I said. Then I assured him that beyond that, I was ignorant, but–and believe me, I *did* say this, though my behavior at home might have belied it at the time–I said I believed he should let it be, let it just die naturally, as I thought it would."

"Not Rupert's way, is it?" Lydia said, biting her lip.

"So you suspect I might have caused even more trouble?"

"If you did, it was unintentional. Besides, what could you do? He approached you demanding information. It wouldn't have helped if you had brushed him off and refused to speak of it; might even have made matters worse."

"Thank you, Lydia."

"What?"

"Thank you for recognizing that I really would not say anything that might hurt Emmeline."

"Oh, Henry, I really have wounded you, haven't I?"

"I was afraid I had lost you."

"Never. Never, never, never. I know your heart."

He gazed at her, and she smiled and then jerked him back to the gravity of her concern.

"What am I to do? Do you think . . .? Well, you know I can't just ignore it. Poor Emmeline is lonely enough at best. Rupert allows her practically no friends, very few visits . . ."

"He tolerates you, though, doesn't he?"

"Only because I won't be denied," she said dryly, and paused before continuing: "And that's the answer, isn't it? Not Madge. Me. I'll drop over myself. Certainly not the first time."

Henry made no protest, whatever his reservations. She was right. It would not be the first of her unannounced visits.

That very afternoon, she fulfilled her pledge. The familiar walk, though considerable, was invigorating in the bracing air of an unusually sunny day. The wild daffodils had already appeared with their graceful yellow audacity, nodding pertly at her from the deep green meadows. They almost made her forget the anxiety that was twisting inside her. She smiled and breathed more deeply of spring's sudden warmth and the twisting abated slightly, but when she reached the Plowhursts' door, she forgot the daffodils, the sunshine, and even forgot that it was spring, feeling momentarily that all her entrails had migrated to her throat. Biting her lip, she quieted her nervousness by knocking briskly.

Though the Plowhursts' situation could accommodate more household servants than Henry could afford, the footman was engaged elsewhere, and Nora, their maid, had to abandon a task in the parlor to answer Lydia's summons. The delay did nothing to ease her anxiety. When Nora finally opened the door, hesitantly, her cheeks colored noticeably.

"Mrs. Glendrake . . ." It was almost a gasp.

"Yes, Nora. You seem surprised."

"No, ma'am. Um . . . Yes . . . No, ma'am. But Mrs. Plow'urst can't see nobody today, ma'am"

"Is she not well?"

Nora hesitated, lowering her eyes. "No'm. Not well at all."

Lydia was sure it was a lie. "When I was ill, Mrs. Plowhurst came to keep me company and tend to my needs. She brought me all the comfort of a cherished friendship. Am I to be denied the chance to return such a gentle favor?"

Nora blushed more deeply and stammered, "I'm . . . I'm sorry Mrs. Glendrake, but I don't 'ave . . . Mr. Plow'urst 'as told me . . . um . . ."

"May I see Mr. Plowhurst, Nora?"

"I dunno, ma'am." She looked frightened.

"Please ask, will you, Nora?"

The girl's eyes darkened with apprehension, then resolve. She lowered them as she murmured, "Yes ma'am," and left the door ajar as she turned and disappeared into the interior, leaving Lydia alone on the step.

Rupert Plowhurst appeared shortly, his face a mask of disapproval, his eyes glinting with intransigence.

"What may I do for you, Mrs. Glendrake?" he asked with frigid courtesy.

"Please let me see Emmeline, Mr. Plowhurst. Surely I can help . . ."

"That's quite impossible, Mrs. Glendrake. She is not well."

"I gathered that. But I can't forget her kindness when I was ill. Her visit meant a great deal to me, and I only wish to return that kindness and bring her what comfort I can."

"It would not be—um—would not be advisable. I'm afraid I must decline your generous offer. Thank you, but she must not be disturbed."

"Is it so serious, then?"

"I have said that company is inadvisable. That is sufficient intelligence concerning the matter. Forgive me, but I must bid you good day."

The door closed incisively, leaving Lydia staring at its indifference to the cruel rebuff its owner had dealt her.

Back on the path toward home, she was now oblivious to the saucy daffodils that had delighted her and lightened her apprehensions a few moments earlier. Their nodding enchantment met with thoughts too heavy for appeasement or distraction, thoughts that swirled about poor Emmeline, too ill to receive her. Her steps took her past the wing that contained Emmeline's bedroom. It was some distance from the path lined by the high wrought-iron fence that surrounded the Plowhurst gardens. Lydia's eyes scanned the window, and she yearned to be inside, holding Emmeline's hand or reading her a soothing tale.

A figure passed the window and then returned immediately, as if drawn by her presence on the path. It was Emmeline. Yes, she was sure, it was she, now standing at the window, disheveled but dressed, looking helplessly through the hermetic pane. She waved, a quick, desperate gesture, and Lydia answered with her own wave and then saw the light change in the room, as though a door had opened, and Emmeline left the window. Shortly, an unknown hand drew the curtains, leaving the room impenetrable as midnight.

Nine

Dinner in Horse Stone House that evening held a solemnity unlike anything since Henry's breach of gentility when he pouted over Lydia's decision to read the Book of Mormon at Emmeline's urging. Noting her reticence, he held his tongue until mealtime was over and they could be alone.

"What is it, love?" he asked tenderly.

Lydia sighed and told him all that had happened at the Plowhursts.

"You're sure it was Emmeline you saw at the window?"

"Yes. It was Emmeline. Who else would it be? It was her bedroom. I've been there; you know I have. I was with her when she suffered the grippe, and Nora took me up to her—to that very room. I know I was not close enough to see her face, but I knew her gesture, her wave. It couldn't have been anyone else."

"I suppose you're right. Don't know what could be going on. Rupert told you she was too ill to receive you, and then you see her up and dressed and waving to you. Not consistent, is it?"

"No. And she was distressed, I know she was. Afraid."

"Well, we'll have to wait."

"Wait? Wait for what?"

"For her to improve, I suppose, if she is ill. Surely she'll contact you."

"She can't. Henry, they–*he* won't release her. He wouldn't let me in and he won't let her out."

"She's a prisoner, then."

"Just the same. That bedroom is her jail. Her wave was—It was as close to a cry as a hand-wave can be."

Henry shook his head, his brow knit in perplexity. "I wonder what—who could . . . Her family, her mother or father . . . ?"

"They might! Yes, they might know something! How soon could we go?"

"Too late this evening. We would be quite inappropriate making a call at this hour. But tomorrow . . . trouble is, I'm not free, unless we wait. I've an appointment."

"I know, Henry. This is something I'll do. And I don't want to wait."

"But you'll need someone to drive you."

"I can drive horses, Henry."

"I know you can. It's not you I worry about. Well, at least not your capability with a team of horses. It's what might be said of you were you to assume the role of coachman. Not seemly, is it? You're a lady. Squire Smirthwaite's daughter, after all. You can't drive your own carriage."

"Oh, bother the whole system. I know I can do it, you know I can do it, even the horses know I can do it!"

"Maybe so, but you also know I can't permit it. Expectations allow only a small margin of independence before I'm considered a threat to decency, and I must consider business."

"Oh, all right. Send one of your apprentices. Hector, maybe. Pay him for his time and he'll leap at the chance. An apprentice wheelwright is hardly overwhelmed with chances for extra money, and he's a decent sort."

"I'll talk to him. You're probably right. Does his best, doesn't he, poor chap."

Hector drove Lydia to the Hamilton farm early the following morning.

"I'll not be more than twenty or thirty minutes, I expect,"

Lydia assured him.

The housemaid answered her knock, smiled her welcome recognition, and ushered her inside.

"I'll tell Mrs. 'Amilton you're 'ere," she said, leaving her to contemplate the furnishings she had come to know as a girl—the comfortable old bookcase, the books dusted carefully but used hardly at all, the inexpensive but comfortable-looking old bureau lined with family photographs that characteristically displayed self-conscious and dour expressions. She smiled furtively. Photographs might record the exact moment of the subject's pose when the photographer finally squeezed the button, but they represented a very poor example of true human essence. Ironically, only by accident did a photographer ever capture any suggestion of spiritual reality or interpretation of character. The necessity of posing for painfully long moments obviated all possibility of genuineness. Yet a photograph of Emmeline, taken sometime in her ninth year, provided the glaring exception. She had smiled at the crucial moment, a beguiling, innocent expression that revealed a childish purity and lack of affectation that had never faded. Lydia blanched. The photograph had always been there, but she had forgotten, and the effect stunned her momentarily. She swallowed to keep her tears at bay and her composure serene. She looked away. Memories of her childhood romps with Emmeline, their playful excursions through the house, their furtive moments in this very room–off limits by decorous decree–invaded her consciousness.

Mrs. Hamilton entered smiling warmly, but a hint of uneasy curiosity lurked in her expression as well.

"Lydia, how kind of you to drop by. It's ever so nice to see you. Makes me think I'm young again." She laughed, a tight little giggle that betrayed her nervousness, and embraced her visitor with ritual affection.

Lydia returned her greeting, declined her offer of tea, and then came directly to the point.

"Mrs. Hamilton, I have been to visit Emmeline and was not permitted audience with her. Mr. Plowhurst insisted that she was much too delicate, and would offer no elucidation to reassure me.

I am quite beside myself to learn the nature and extent of her misfortune."

Mrs. Hamilton's expression tightened and the slight wariness deepened.

"I know very little, my dear. I'm afraid I . . . Perhaps I shouldn't say."

"But you know something, surely. Mrs. Hamilton, you must know how deeply I feel for Emmeline. I have never threatened to use my connections to pry into matters that do not concern me, but Emmeline is my dearest friend; her welfare concerns me most urgently, and if I can learn nothing here, I shall pursue whatever avenue I must to gain the intelligence that satisfies me. If you can help me—and I think you can—please save me the bother of searching elsewhere."

Mrs. Hamilton's wariness softened a little. "Rupert—Mr. Plowhurst—disapproves of Emmeline's . . . well, she seems to have found a religion that I . . . I wish I could tell you I understand her. I don't, Lydia. She's a God-fearing girl, and to take up with blasphemers . . . It makes no sense."

"Blasphemers, Mrs. Hamilton?"

"You don't know. It's a religion that believes God is not the same as Christ, but Christ is God, and so is His Father. And the Holy Ghost—*three* Gods, Lydia! Now I ask you . . . We're Christians, true Christians, and that means we worship *one* God!" She began to weep. "Oh, Emmeline, Emmeline . . ."

Lydia touched her arm comfortingly.

"Why can I not see her, Mrs. Hamilton?"

"He won't let her go. He's holding her in her room." She wiped her eyes. "I've tried to see her myself, but he . . . Oh, I know poor Rupert is only trying to make her see . . . to be reasonable. But shutting her away like that . . ."

Lydia's flushed face betrayed the anger that boiled inside her, but she did her best to keep her voice level.

"It's quite intolerable, Mrs. Hamilton. Emmeline must be released. Why haven't you—why hasn't your husband asserted himself?"

"Lydia, dear, Emmeline is a married woman. A man and his wife are not divided in our law, and Rupert is her husband. I suppose he is being as responsible as he can be, given his views. He's after all trying to protect her from the folly of a false religion."

"And what right has he—or have you, or I—to decide for another human being how to worship God? Especially when the decision that's made for her is made in ignorance!"

"Lydia..."

"Because it *is*, isn't it? Ignorance! Have you listened to Emmeline, Mrs. Hamilton? No, of course you haven't. You did just what I did when she came to me for friendly understanding. I rejected her, without study or contemplation. She was, by my own pre-determination, wrong. And I'm sure she has had no sympathetic audience from Rupert, has she? And now, because she wants to worship God as her own conscience guides her, she is to be shut away and left frightfully alone. Mustn't have an inappropriate church about, must we? Much more proper in our highly civilized society to force everyone into the mold *we* have fashioned."

Mrs. Hamilton stiffened. Her eyes hardened, but she could not answer the challenge in Lydia's own steady gaze, and she looked away. Her lips tightened and barely moved as she answered, "It is not for me or for Mr. Hamilton to interfere in what our laws condone. Rupert will deal with the matter as he thinks fitting, and as I'm sure you must recognize, your views of Emmeline's circumstances are immaterial."

"Immaterial? Emmeline is imprisoned in her own house, denied converse or association with any but her gaolers, and my outrage is immaterial? Thank you, Mrs. Hamilton, for your courageous concern. I will trouble you no further."

She turned her back on Mrs. Hamilton's confusion and marched with stiff dignity to where Hector awaited her in her carriage.

As Henry listened, perplexity knitted a scowl across his face. Lydia's account troubled him, especially as he contemplated her strong tendency to fly in the face of convention when her sense of fair play was challenged, and he had to consider his own outrage at Rupert's cruel reaction to Emmeline's innocent if unconventional religious leanings. Yet he remembered his own sullen response to Lydia's peripheral though sympathetic involvement with her friend's convictions and wondered if he had a right to judge the man. Lydia was sure to act, try to find a way of securing Emmeline's release, of that he was certain, and he searched through all his thoughts to discover what might be done. He silently wished he could be free of the wretched muddle, but he too worried about Emmeline's situation. She had never seemed particularly strong, but she had always been so pleasant, so congenial. He could not imagine anyone, least of all the girl's husband, wishing her ill or intentionally mistreating her. If she was indeed held prisoner in her own home, it was inexcusable, a cruelty beyond tolerance. Yet what could he do? Emmeline's own mother had essentially declined involvement on her behalf.

Henry had already confirmed the results of Lydia's encounter with Mrs. Hamilton. Henry's father had been a long-time friend to Howard Hamilton, Emmeline's father, and Henry had known him all his life. But for the difference in their ages, their relationship would have admitted of first-name familiarity; Henry, of course, would indulge in no such breach of respect, but each was warmly disposed toward the other. A day or two after Lydia's visit to the Hamilton farm, he met Howard Hamilton in Eccleston and greeted him cheerfully. They talked of inconsequential things—balancing a wheelwright's business with farming, the current prices on wool and other farm products, and finally Henry felt he had plied Mr. Hamilton's volubility enough to broach the topic of his daughter's welfare. He asked directly, with not the slightest tone of urgency or unwarranted intrusion, his manner as casual as if the topic were no more important than a comment on the weather or the time of day. "Mr. Hamilton, Lydia and I have heard something of Emmeline's situation, and I'm sure you know it distresses us. Can you tell me what's going on? If we can help in some way . . ."

He saw the change in Hamilton's expression, a change so subtle it was all but imperceptible.

"Yes, Henry. Agnes spoke to me of Lydia's concern—her visit at home. It may be that my daughter's situation has only one solution. Rupert may seem a hard man, but I have asked myself what I would do in his place. I don't suppose I could be cruel—cruel enough to imprison her—but perhaps his firm measures are the only way to bring her to her good sense and Christian up-bringing. What happened to the girl is beyond all reasonable comprehension, and I am powerless to intervene."

"But surely, it does seem—um—excessive to shut her away. She is not a criminal or a . . . lunatic . . ."

"Is she not? I don't know. Can one who is capable of healthy thought suddenly abandon all sense of propriety and meddle with blasphemers and reprobates? Did you know that she pretended illness on more than one occasion and slipped away to attend the services they hold in Eccleston? They hold them in a warehouse on Sundays, and they have weekday meetings in the homes of their misguided proselytes. A warehouse! Something evil has possessed her, Henry. Pure evil!"

"Emmeline? Last I saw her, she seemed as gentle and inoffensive as ever she was. She just doesn't . . . the word evil just doesn't fit with her."

Hamilton wilted. "No. You're right, and it tears at my soul to say it. But what she has done . . ."

"What *has* she done, sir?"

"I told you. She has taken up with a church, some devilish cult."

"The history of the world proves men capable of worshiping God in diverse ways, sir. Why should Emmeline be denied the privilege of her own conscience?"

"Don't try to excuse her! History is also full of fiendish rogues and charlatans! Like that raving American prophet that has somehow lured her fancy and raped her mind!"

Hamilton was breathing hard and his face was flushed. Henry sensed the futility of further argument. He answered softly, "I am sorry, sir. Truly sorry. For Emmeline especially. If she is deranged, I should think that incarceration and harshness will only make matters worse."

"I don't know, Henry. I don't know. As I said, it wouldn't be my choice either, but I am not her husband and it is out of my hands. I refuse to cut across Rupert's decisions."

Henry's disappointment drove him to visit the Woodplumpton police station, where he finally obtained audience with the superintendent. He explained his concern, carefully describing all the events that had urged him to consult the matter with the law. The superintendent listened attentively, asking questions for clarity and accuracy. He was a tall man, lean and slender, with angular features that swindled his face of classic symmetry but endowed it with firmness and character. He seemed genuinely sympathetic.

"Shameful. Abominable behavior. Can't abide the kind of coward who would abuse a poor woman that way. The worst of it is, the law can't reach him. Nothing we can do."

"Nothing . . . What the devil do you mean, nothing you can do?"

"She is his wife. A man and his wife are one in our law, but as you must know, it's not a yoke of equals."

"It well should be."

"The husband votes for her, keeps her. He's responsible for her provender, shelter, and by long tradition, he determines what her religion shall be. His social status may depend in large measure on her recognizing that. If she is fed, clothed, and sheltered, we cannot enjoin the methods he chooses to persuade her obedience. What I am saying, sir, is that you have just cause for concern but no legal basis for our intervention. No crime has been committed."

Henry stared at the man, a man of authority who clearly acknowledged the outrage, yet was helpless to offer a remedy. Henry excused himself politely, walked to his waiting carriage and rode home in silence, listening to the slow, hollow staccato of the horse's hooves that seemed to drum frustration deeper inside him with each indifferent step.

Ten

Madge could see agony in Lydia's eyes whenever she spoke of Emmeline, and when the situation became clear to her and she herself felt the cruel injustice heaped upon a woman whose crime was to adopt an inappropriate creed, she surrendered all her sympathy to Emmeline and all her angry resentment fell to Rupert. She felt an overwhelming need to help Lydia in her quest to save Emmeline and restore to her the freedom to perceive God as she chose and find Him where she might. It did not seem at all mysterious to Madge that Emmeline had not found Him in Rupert's church.

Her childhood had given her no training in religious practice of any sort. One old crone who lived in the same crowded tenement from which her mother had been evicted intoned endless warnings of God's displeasure and assured most everyone that passed that way that they were all bound for hell. It did little to dispose little Madge toward God or persuade her of His mercy. She had never prayed, and the few whom she knew that did seemed no better off than the others as they struggled with the same feeble resources that had divested her of her only family. In her present security, she remembered the hunger and cold, implacable and endless, the ruthlessness of the collectors and most of the street urchins whose own desperation spawned suspicion and brutality and rarely allowed for a generous gesture. The acts of kindness were so few, perhaps because hunger gave no quarter, allowed no time for gentleness, and yet she remembered Miles Fernley, the tavern keeper, who permitted her to feed on scraps that customers had left on their plates. Even in that inferno where she was born, God's goodness had its agents.

She felt a strange blend of relief and lingering concern for the ones who still lived as she had lived–dirty, desperate, hopeless. Her loyalty to Lydia and Henry almost consumed her. She learned of God through their devotions and believed in Him because they did. Her prayers, such as they were, were prayers for Lydia and Henry, mostly silent, and prayers of gratitude. She heard Lydia teaching her children, heard Henry read them Bible stories and explain them in patiently modified language. And Madge followed the family to church. There she heard sermons that left her squirming and even sparked an occasional desire to argue. The vicar's voice carried a woeful, wheedling sing-song cadence, and she wished that Henry might somehow replace him. The ritual of the service left her quite indifferent, yet when Lydia talked of God in her home, to her children or to Madge, or taught them to pray, or when Henry read them the Bible stories, she felt oddly fulfilled. God became a reality, but He lived at home, not at church.

Lydia often confided in little Madge, for whom she had forged a protective affection that she could never have imagined when she first manipulated a position for her in her mother's house. As days went by and her efforts to discover a solution for Emmeline appeared more and more futile, she became irritable and weepy in pure frustration. Madge approached her a bit fearfully:

"Could I 'elp, ma'am? I knows Nora a bit. Sees 'er wen I buys fings at the market. She's a good girl, she is, and I know she in't 'appy wiv wot's 'appenin' at 'er 'ouse, coz I seen 'er cryin' an' I axed 'er, curious-like and wantin' to 'elp if I could, wot was 'er trouble, and she said it was nuffin' as anyone could do, but she was fearful for 'er mistress."

"Was that all she said?"

"Yes, ma'am. I knew it wasn't no sickness as troubled 'er mistress. But I was bein' polite-like, and I axed 'er if 'er lady was ailin' much and in pain, and she says to me, 'Not ailin',' in the usual way, not 'er. Ailin' in 'er 'eart, she is, poor woman.' She wou'nt say no more."

"Madge, you know Nora's market schedule, don't you?"

"Yes ma'am. She 'as a reg'lar time of Mondays and Wen'sdys. Other times don't 'ave no schedule to 'em, but Mondays and Wen'sdys she goes early, first thing, same as me."

Lydia smiled. Madge insisted on doing her market purchases while selections were fresh. It was her own choice, not one they imposed upon her.

"Do you feel you can trust Nora, Madge? To help Emmeline? I mean, if she could?"

"Oh, yes, ma'am. She don't 'old no good feelings for old Plow'urst, she don't. 'E's a 'ard one, 'e is."

"I'm going to write her a note. Do you think Nora could deliver it without Mr. Plowhurst's notice?"

"Oh, she could, ma'am. Nora'll 'elp 'er if she can, yes ma'am." Her eyes glistened with the joy of Lydia's confidence and her own sense of usefulness.

Lydia hastily penned her message:

Dearest Emmeline:

    I trust Nora. She has always seemed level-headed, and Madge tells me she feels deep concern for you, so I am sending our Madge to your Nora with this note. I tried to see you, as I'm sure you know, but was told that you were too delicate for visitors; yet I saw you wave to me from your window as I was returning home. I also paid a visit to your mother, who revealed the truth of your situation, leaving me deeply troubled to discover a remedy. For the moment, I can find none, but be assured, I will do all I can to alter conditions and secure your release. In the meantime, please take courage. I know this must be dreadful for you.

    Your dearest friend,
    Lydia

Placing Lydia's note carefully at the bottom of her shopping basket, Madge set out for the market with a posture stiffer than usual, a glance more resolute, a step more firm. Her minute frame, her scrawny limbs, and her entire demeanor had assumed a military dignity.

She arrived at the gate of the marketplace and looked about for Nora. Assuring herself that she had preceded her, she made a few routine purchases, always with her eye roving to be sure she did not miss Nora's arrival. She began to grow nervous as minutes dragged on, but was finally rewarded with the glimpse of Nora's familiar swaying step as she spotted her just entering the market. She abandoned her errands and rushed to meet her.

"Nora! Me mistress 'as writ a letter as must be took to Mrs. Plow'urst!" she blurted even before Nora could consider the formality of a greeting.

"A letter? I cou'nt give 'er nuffink like that, Madge. Mr. Plow'urst is 'arder than the devil's own 'eart, 'e is, and set as 'e is on 'avin' 'is way, 'e'd put me out wivout blinkin' 'is bloomin' eye, evil as it is."

"Then yer'll 'ave t'be frightful careful 'e don't 'ave no notion of it, won't yer?" Madge said with an edge that meant challenge. "If 'e's evil as yer say, somebody 'as to take Mrs. Plow'urst's part, says I, and 'ave the spine fer it wivout shrinkin'. My mistress in't goin' to allow 'is poor missus to stay shut up like that, maybe starve . . ."

"Oh, she in't starvin', I sees to that. I brings 'er food and the like, but 'e won't 'ave 'er speakin' to nobody, not till she comes to 'er senses, as 'e says."

"If yer brings food to 'er, yer could slip a little note wiv it. Under a cup or sumfin'."

Nora looked dubious, but Madge could see that she was wavering.

"Yer could 'av a bit of a spark in yer own way, knowin' as 'ow yer'd 'elped the poor woman."

Nora bit her lip. It was dangerous. She could be dismissed. Yes, such insubordination would not be forgiven, not in Rupert Plowhurst's household. Yet the thought of putting one over on him and helping to ease the distress of her gentle mistress was too delicious to deny. The outrage he was perpetrating filled her with loathing, and more than once she had cursed her impotence. She began to relish the thought that even in her lowly station she might actually have a hand in her mistress's liberation, and the sweetness of it made it worth the risk. She nodded, and her expression carried resolution. Madge smiled, seeing her confidence and decisiveness. It was full complicity now. She reached to the bottom of her basket, placed Lydia's note in Nora's hand, and watched as she tucked it carefully in her own basket. As she began to move on with her shopping duties, Madge said,

"I'll see yer next Wen'sdy. Bless yer, Nora."

When Wednesday finally arrived, Madge made her early way to the market again with the excitement of adventure pounding in her bosom. The routine of her chores was all but forgotten, and the only really important matter was Emmeline. Again, she had arrived before Nora, but only a trifle. Nora appeared, eager and breathless, before she had time to buy anything.

"I gave me lady the letter," Nora said beaming. "It were easy, and Mr. Plow'urst di'nt see nuffink. She read it, all excited-like, and cried a little, poor soul. She wrote 'er answer right then, and I brung it!"

Reaching into her shopping bag, she drew out a sealed envelope. Madge took it gingerly and tucked it into the pocket of her apron. Then yielding to a poignant urge, she threw her arms about Nora, whose startle lasted only an instant before she answered with her own embrace. The two girls used no words, just giggles of complicity. Then each set about dutifully answering the demands of their respective responsibilities, selecting produce with critical competence.

Home again, Madge delivered the letter to Lydia, momentarily forgetting the market produce she had brought.

"It's a letter, ma'am. Fum Mrs. Plow'urst, what Nora brung for us, just like we thought!" She was trembling with excitement and savoring her role in the conspiracy and her own importance as a messenger.

"Thank you, Madge. I'm so glad." In her excitement, Lydia's words came tumbling from her in jerks. "I was so hoping . . . and she did . . . we got our message to her, didn't we? Thank you," she repeated. They were in the kitchen. She looked at the letter, tempted to tear the envelope hastily away and get to the heart of the matter. She turned to go to the withdrawing room but sensed Madge's eagerness to share the rewards of her own efforts. Lydia seized a kitchen knife and quickly slit the envelope with a decisive whisk and then removed the contents with trembling fingers. Madge kept a respectful distance but could not hide her impatience. Lydia struggled with the thought of the need for privacy. The letter was not meant for her maid, but for her, yet Madge had done all the leg-work, and she could not in fairness exclude her from this moment. She quickly scanned the letter to verify that it contained nothing she needed to withhold, sat at the kitchen table, and read aloud:

> Dearest Lydia:
>
> I must tell you that your little note, smuggled to me by my blessed Nora, saved me from utter despair. I am not permitted to leave my room. Rupert locks the door and pockets the key. Nora is allowed entrance only to clean and bring me nourishment, and I treasure her company. She would release me if she could, but no one, I fear, can accomplish that.
>
> I did see you, as you mentioned, the day you came to visit me, and I tried to communicate with you, but all I could manage was a quick wave before Rupert entered and drew the curtains. I have been desolate since.
>
> I am assured that all I need do to secure my release is renounce my affiliation with the Mormons. You know that I am not by nature rebellious. I have been an obedient daughter, a compliant wife. Now I have discovered God. I have always believed in Him, but now I begin to know Him. I have met with

people who believe, and I love their company. I have felt a peace I have never known before, and I feel that I have found truth, the pure truth of God's love and His restored kingdom. I now must choose between my faith and my husband, and perhaps my parents. I can no longer be a submissive subject to others' views. I must have the courage of my own faith.

You will remember my asking you why God no longer speaks to us. He does, Lydia. I have not heard the actual timbre of His voice, but I have heard His message. It has reached my heart, and I must not deny it. How can I reject my God after I have finally found Him? It would be more comfortable to do what Rupert demands, but I would be even more miserable than he has made me with this isolation. I can't—I mustn't—deny what I know I have been given.

Please pray for me. I don't know what else can be done, but pray that God will give me courage.

Could you, perhaps, contact Brother Kimball? He's the missionary who taught me, you remember. Heber is his Christian name. You will find him meeting with the Saints—I mean the members of his congregation—on Sundays, in Eccleston. They meet in a warehouse on Parr Lane, close to the Sherbourn tannery. He will be grieved, I know, but tell him why I can no longer meet with them, and perhaps his prayers may be added to yours for my delivery. I pray that he is still there. I know he must move on sometime soon.

If you can please send me more letters, Nora will see that I get them. How I have come to treasure her!

Yours most affectionately,
Emmeline

Madge was sniffling as Lydia finished reading. She turned without a word and left the kitchen, and Lydia sat alone at the table, her gaze frozen in space, the letter held loosely between her fingers on her lap, her thoughts as unfocused as her eyes. She was still in that posture when Henry walked in.

"Hello, my dear? What . . . ?"

Lydia seemed to awaken from a trance.

"Henry! I was . . . lost, I suppose. Thinking of Emmeline, but without any kind of thought that could suggest a solution. Read."

"Read?"

"Yes. Read her letter." She handed it to him.

"A letter? How . . ."

"I wrote her a note and sent it with Madge to give to Nora to give to Emmeline. She answered. Read."

He frowned, taking the page, and read it quickly. He handed it back.

"No surprises. We knew, didn't we?"

"Yes, we did, but hearing it from her makes it so . . . so awfully immediate. So hopeless."

"Can't lose hope. I suppose we can visit this . . . this minister?"

"Of course. But what can he do? Emmeline's own parents can't–or won't–help, the police can't intervene, we're not allowed to come near her . . ." her voice trailed away.

"Sunday's only four days away. We'll go to Eccleston. Meantime, send her another note."

"Can't until Monday. That's when Nora goes to market again. Maybe by then—after we talk with Mr. Kimball . . ."

"Yes, we'll talk to him. At least we can tell her we have seen him. Give her that small satisfaction. Assure her that we have done what we could."

The next day, Madge moved through her routine with about as much energy as could be coaxed from a distempered cab mare, and Lydia herself could boast little more enthusiasm. The children grew irritable in the unusually tense atmosphere. Henry left for work in the morning solemnly taciturn, explaining that he would not be able to return until evening. At midday, as they were feeding the little ones, Lydia noted how appetites had fallen off, and she realized with a jolt that the whole household had grown morose. Madge's silence, the pinched line where her smile used to be, the sullen eyes that had lost their sparkle, the children's tears that erupted readily, no doubt in response to the stress they could not fathom, convinced her of the mute desperation that had invaded them—evidence of how deeply Emmeline's plight had affected them all. She straightened her posture and affected a smile, struggling for a lighter mood.

"Madge, dear, after dinner let's sit quietly with the children. Read to them, perhaps. Or we can go to the piano for a few songs. We're about to burst with distress, as though we were ourselves victims."

"I just can't think on 'er wivout 'urtin' inside me, ma'am. It's worse than 'avin' to go back to the tenements."

"I know. But we can't help her by wallowing in misery and making life miserable for the children, can we?"

"No, ma'am. But I ain't . . . I ain't ever thought of bein' shut away wivout seein' nuffink but the four walls what's 'oldin' me in. I been 'ungry and I been cold, but I ain't never been shut away."

"Henry and I are going to see Emmeline's minister next Sunday. I don't suppose he'll be able to help, but we'll be sure to do what we can."

Madge's eyes widened. "Yer goin' to 'er church, ma'am?"

"No, we're just going to visit her pastor. She wants us to, you remember."

"Yes, but—it's on Sunday yer goin' in't it? The day yer goes to the church where the vicar does 'is preachin'."

"I suppose we'll miss the vicar's sermon this Sunday."

"Um . . . could I come wiv yer, ma'am? I'll 'elp yer wiv the little ones, same as when we go to yer usual church." Church was always "your" church, as she laid only tenuous, indirect claim upon it.

"I see no reason why you shouldn't come if you want to. Of course. The experience probably won't do the children any harm. Of course you may come."

Eleven

They arrived without any notion of schedule. They had no way of determining what time Emmeline's church began services, but assumed they would convene at a mid-morning hour. Henry knew the area and quickly located Parr Lane and the warehouse near Sherbourne tannery. The movement of a few people toward the entrance to the sagging, weather-worn structure assured them that they had found the right place, and the time appeared propitious. Lydia and Madge, with the children in tow, got off the carriage as near the entrance as Henry could drive. Then he proceeded on to where a few other carriages and teams were tethered.

Lydia and Madge stopped at the entrance to wait for Henry. Lydia felt oddly self-conscious and uncomfortable despite the warmth of the sunny morning. The people who were entering smiled and greeted them cheerfully. Some seemed eager to engage them further, but Lydia maintained a stiff posture, gave a polite but non-committal nod, and put on a tight, chilly little smile that invited no familiarity. Most of the parishioners, if that's what they called themselves, got the message and moved on. She wished to make it clear that she stood aloof from their convictions and was quite satisfied with her own. One man, either possessed of irrepressible affability or too obtuse to recognize dismissal, apparently did not grasp her separatist inclinations.

"Good morning, sisters. How can I be of service to you?"

Lydia thought his manner was unctuous. Her eyebrows arched over a glacial glare that might have frozen the landscape. Her smile, like painted politeness, did not conceal the deprecation she intended and her voice crowned her intent with a tone so icy as to convince a drunken cretin. She had grown up as gentry and knew the language of intimidation.

"Thank you. We're waiting for my husband."

The man's volubility wilted, and he dismissed himself with a wan smile and a weak nod. Madge looked with open incredulity at her mistress. The man had not provoked such a peremptory reaction, and she had never seen rudeness so blatant in her mistress. Lydia caught the dismay in Madge's face and blanched slightly. With growing shame, she realized that she was behaving with the same prejudice she had expressed when Emmeline first told her of her interest in a new doctrine, and had yielded to the same snobbery that she had always criticized in her own class, the kind of exclusiveness that would have made her marriage to Henry impossible. Yet at this moment, she felt tainted by being there. She blushed in confusion. She suddenly remembered how her reading of the Book of Mormon had surprised her, and then she remembered Emmeline, whose conviction had given her courage to hold out against her husband's tyranny and slip away to come here, to this warehouse, to worship with these very people from whom Lydia was withdrawing.

Henry's arrival cut across her frustration. She took his arm and they started in just as a young man passed them. Henry stopped him.

"Pardon me, sir, I'm looking to speak with Mr. Kimball. Heber, I believe, is his Christian name. Do you know him?"

The young man grinned broadly. "Yes, sir, I knows 'im. 'E'll be startin' the meetin' now. That's 'im standin' there be'ind 'is pulpit. If yer wantin' t' meet 'im, after the services I'll take yer to 'im. Introduce yer." He seemed pleased with his importance.

Henry nodded indifferently. He had not intended to stay for services, but apparently he had delayed a bit too long with his carriage and horses. They entered. The "chapel" was a large storage area that had been partially vacated, with the stored items pushed toward the back and occupying half the space. The other half was cleanly swept, where a small congregation sat on benches improvised with long boards resting on overturned buckets or stacked bricks. In front of them were four large sacks, weighing perhaps one hundred pounds apiece and stacked to a height of about four and a half feet. This was the preacher's "pulpit," behind which stood a balding gentleman with heavy side whiskers, wearing a hint of an ironic smile. The same glint of irony danced in his small, expressive eyes. He was tall, probably three inches taller than Henry, who measured a respectable five feet nine inches. Mr. Kimball's dark coat fit him perfectly, but his physique seemed too robust for containment, giving the impression of boundless vigor and energy.

"Brothers and sisters, I welcome you here. These surroundings, as you can see, aren't up to much, but they're not what drives the spirit of this meeting." His voice had a pleasant somberness but was tinged with the same cordial irony that characterized his smile. Henry and Lydia were trying to get the children settled with Madge doing her best to help, but even with her attention divided, Madge noted the difference between this voice, so artlessly congenial, and the vicar's with its practiced cadence and carefully formed syllables.

"Many of you are already familiar with these make-do facilities. Many of you are here for the first time. All are welcome, and what we say today will apply to all of us. The dusty atmosphere of this place has no importance at all, and if you will lend me the attention of your spirits, you will not mind the rough benches or the stifling temperature of this old building. Just imagine what it will feel like when it turns cold—which it should any minute now, if your fickle English climate holds true to form." A little ripple of laughter greeted his quip. "But for now, if you men are uncomfortable, you can do what I'm going to do . . . ." He peeled off his coat and draped it over the back of a chair behind him. "No need to make things any more disagreeable than necessary."

Henry looked at Lydia, quizzically, as if she should tell him whether he had heard right. She smiled and shrugged.

A few of the men, two or three, wore very rustic trousers and heavy shoes, no doubt their best attire, but no coat. A few others, wearing coats, smiled and removed them. Others sat stoically clad in theirs, with no intention of any such breach of propriety. Henry hesitated and then removed his a little self-consciously, and Madge let a tiny chirp of pleasure escape. Her experience with Sunday meetings had introduced her to a stifling formality she had not fully assimilated.

Brother Kimball, the preacher, announced a hymn and then assigned another man, seated behind the makeshift pulpit, to lead the congregation. With no hymnals, the result was less than angelic harmony, though the hymn was not unfamiliar. Then Brother Kimball announced that they would prepare and serve the sacrament bread and wine, explaining that baptized members should receive them. Henry and Lydia, puzzled at first, gathered that the sacrament bread and wine was the Mormon equivalent of the Eucharist. Kimball and the other missionary–the one who had directed the singing–performed the ceremony at a small table, breaking the bread into small fragments on a pair of plates and then offering a prayer over it. Then the two missionaries carried the plates to the congregation. Henry and Lydia noticed that some ate and others did not. When the plate reached their row, Henry and Lydia declined and the children looked puzzled, as did Madge. The young man who had promised to introduce Henry to Brother Kimball quietly took a fragment and passed the plate on. When all had either accepted or declined the offering, the two missionaries–Mr. Kimball and the other one whom Henry and Lydia dismissed because as far as they knew he had nothing to do with Emmeline–then blessed a goblet of wine and circulated it as they had the bread, with some taking a ritual sip and some declining. They gathered that those declining were curious onlookers, like themselves, or unbaptized proselytes.

After the sacrament ceremony, Mr. Kimball stood again behind his sack-pulpit, a pair of books resting on the pulpit top. He appeared quite at ease, never losing that cordial air of irony and reserved familiarity.

"Brothers and sisters, as you can tell from my American twang, I don't count among my gifts a fine education. I reckon I sound to you a little like a banjo among the instruments of a fine orchestra, or maybe worse. And I don't count riches—worldly riches, at least—among my qualifications. Many of you know already that I'm here because I have a commission, and it's not from the president of the United States. My commission comes from a higher source. The Queen of England couldn't bestow this commission on me. No, not even her." Henry smiled, remembering how the vicar used to correct him for that kind of faulty diction, but he liked the missionary's forthrightness and friendly manner, so free of affectation.

"Let me tell you again, if you've heard my story before, or if you haven't, then hear it. It bears repeating, anyway. I mean the story of my commission, how I came to receive i t. . ."

Later, neither Henry nor Lydia could have traced with exactness the trajectory of Brother Kimball's sermon, but both could remember that his commission was the holy priesthood, and his sermon explained carefully where it had come from. Heavenly messengers, resurrected agents of the Lord, had restored it—a priesthood lost through error and ignorance—and restored as well the ancient organization of Christ's church, with convincing biblical indications both of its original structure and its predicted disappearance and ultimate return. He ended his sermon by affirming the divine source of his authority and his personal assurance that God had spoken to him through spiritual communication to validate his ordination. Then he promised that each person, every child of God, could receive the same spiritual confirmation of the truth.

"I am a man. My arm is made of flesh. You have heard my testimony, and you know, even as you hear my voice at this moment, that I speak what I know in my heart to be true, but you can't know that it's true through me. If you rely only on the arm of flesh, you will live in a fool's paradise for a time and then wind up disappointed. God has His agents here, good men and true, and I hope to qualify as one of them, but I would never advise you to take my word alone on this matter or any other matter as important as your relationship with God. Your only sure path is to ask God Himself. He is the source of truth, and if I speak the truth, He will confirm it for you. So ask Him. Not me. Not your vicar, whose arm, like mine, is made of flesh. Not your friend, not your priest, not even your mother. All of these will have an opinion. Oh, I don't doubt for an instant that they will have opinions, and will share them freely, but only God can give you a reliable answer if you go to Him with faith and sincerity. He's the only One you can always confide in with the perfect understanding that He will not deceive you. I can be deceived. I am susceptible to error. God is not. Remember that, and go to Him."

The total sermon lasted for over an hour. The children were restless, Madge was wide-eyed and silent, Henry and Lydia thoughtful. Brother Kimball invited his companion to speak, and they learned his name: Brother Amos Fielding. The children began to protest. Among the three adult caretakers, they managed to quiet them somewhat. Fortunately, Brother Fielding's sermon was brief—a reaffirmation of the restoration mentioned by Brother Kimball, all in the name of the Lord. A hymn followed, and it was no improvement over the earlier one. A member from the congregation was invited to pray, bringing the meeting to its close.

The young man who had offered to introduce Henry seemed to forget, as he hurriedly engaged a young lady in conversation, apparently fearful that she would leave before he could catch her attention. Henry did not mind; in fact, he felt relieved to be able to introduce himself. What he had to say was not to be shared with anyone but Mr. Kimball. Lydia and Madge stayed with the children while Henry approached the small group surrounding Kimball. When he finally could speak with him privately, he moved forward.

"Mr. Kimball, I'm Henry Glendrake. I'm here because . . ."

"Very glad you are, Mr. Glendrake. How can I help you?"

"I'm concerned about one of your parishioners . . ."

"I have no parish, Mr. Glendrake. I'm not a professional clergyman. At least, I'm not paid for what I do."

"Well, it's one of your proselytes . . ."

"One of our members. Yes. Which one?"

"Emmeline Plowhurst, sir."

"Emmeline. Yes. I have wondered about her. I met her at one of our street meetings here in town. She stopped to listen, and after the meeting I gave her a Book of Mormon. Then she started attending services with us whenever she could. Her husband's not friendly."

"You're likely not aware of how broadly you understate the situation, sir. He's about as friendly as a pack of starving timber wolves. That's why I'm here. Emmeline's a prisoner in her own house, held there to keep her from any communion with you or your . . . I'm sorry, I suppose they're not parishioners. What did you say they are?"

"They're my brothers and sisters, sir. We're members of God's restored church."

"Well, yes. Anyway, that's Emmeline's situation. She smuggled a letter to my wife through her maid and asked if we would communicate with you to let you know why she could not join with your congregation."

Lydia had by now ushered her children outside with Madge, who would give them the opportunity to walk off some of their peevishness after sitting still so long in the stuffy warehouse, and had come to join Henry and meet Mr. Kimball. She heard Henry's last explanation and saw the preacher's face grow suddenly grave, his smile giving way to a scowl. He said nothing for a time, lowering his eyes and then raised his head again, his concern still etched in his expression.

"Thank you for bringing me her message, sir. I'm sorry. Could you tell me, please, how I might reach her husband?"

Henry grimaced slightly. "I wouldn't advise approaching him, Mr. Kimball. He is in no mood to receive you."

"I'm quite used to that mood. It doesn't intimidate me."

Lydia chimed in with muted but definite alarm, without the formality of an introduction: "But you could make things more difficult for Emmeline, sir."

The preacher turned toward her smiling.

"Your wife, Mr. Glendrake?"

Henry nodded and was on the verge of making the introduction more formal, but Mr. Kimball anticipated him.

"I'm pleasured to know you, sister," he said, bowing politely.

Lydia winced imperceptibly. He had addressed her as "sister," a title she imagined was reserved for members of his flock. She smiled and added, "I have known Emmeline—oh, probably all my life. I went to see her and was refused admittance. Mr. Plowhurst masked his rudeness with protocol politeness but couldn't have been nastier with a textbook to guide him. I doubt he would indulge you with even the show of politeness, sir. Your presence could be his excuse to make greater hardship than ever for his wife. That's not just an idle concern, it's a genuine possibility."

"Yes, I see." He cast a quick look toward a man and wife waiting at the entrance with Mr. Fielding, his companion missionary. "We need to discuss this further. I am totally unwilling–unable, even—to dismiss it. Mrs. Plowhurst is a dear lady, deserving of the kindest and gentlest consideration, and I will do what I can, though I certainly can't imagine at the moment what that might be. Right now, I have to keep another promise. Brother and Sister Fell are waiting for me, with Elder Fielding. We're going to their home to give a priesthood blessing to young Dilworth, their son, who's suffering with what appears to be pneumonia. After I have visited them and given him God's blessing, I hope I may visit your house in the early evening. Would that be convenient?"

"Of course," Henry said immediately, not allowing his surprise to supersede courtesy. He explained where Horse Stone House was located, the exact road to take, and the landmarks to follow.

"That's–what? Four or five miles from here?" Mr. Kimball asked, with a look of embarrassed disappointment.

"Yes. We arrived at your services a bit behind schedule. I either started too late or drove too slowly. But had we been able to speak with you before services started, the chances are rather good that we would not have stayed to hear your interesting sermon."

Mr. Kimball smiled, the irony now dancing furiously in his eyes. "You think I would not have had enough persuasiveness to convince you to stay?"

"Well, as for that, I can't say. You might have influenced us, but we did not come with that intention."

Mr. Kimball laughed aloud. "You're a forthright man, Mr. Glendrake. I must be the same. The fact is, I won't be able to reach Horse Stone House this evening. I had imagined you lived closer. I won't be able to walk from the Fells' place all the way to Horse Stone and return to our quarters in Woodplumpton before two o'clock in the morning."

"Woodplumpton?"

"Yes, that's where we're staying."

"If you could manage to come right away, you could accompany us in the carriage. If I were alone, of course I would wait for you, but with the ladies and the children . . ."

"No, that's not possible. I'm unable to predict how long our visit will last. I intend to spend whatever time is necessary at the Fells'. But by tomorrow afternoon . . . Could you receive us then?"

"Yes, but Woodplumpton is almost twelve miles from Horse Stone House."

"I know. It will take us a large portion of the day to get there. And then of course we must think of getting back to Woodplumpton."

"You will surely hire a cab. For a little extra . . ."

"Well, I'm afraid that's the trouble. We're here in answer to the Lord's call, but neither we nor the prophet who made the call have funds for anything extra. We have to take what we can get when it's offered and let shoe leather absorb the brunt of our travel needs. But we can make the trip tomorrow, and quite conveniently, if you will allow us to sleep tomorrow night in your barn."

"In my barn? Well, now, I've spent many a night there myself, but only with a foaling mare or a pregnant cow. It's not the place for a guest. There's room in Horse Stone for you." He reached into his pocket and produced a shilling "This will pay for cab fare. We will expect you in time for dinner at 7:00." He felt a rush of satisfaction when he saw the expression of surprise on the face of this unflappable American for whom he felt a reluctant but undeniable affinity.

"Sir, I accept your very generous offer."

"Then I will expect you tomorrow, and I will delay you no longer today," Henry said, taking Lydia's arm.

She was smiling but quite startled at Henry's impetuous invitation to this stranger with his engaging openness. He was preaching things that people were calling blasphemous, and they were giving him hospice in their own house.

Henry too was a little puzzled at himself as he whisked Lydia away before Mr. Kimball had time to recover his aplomb. He had responded quite spontaneously, almost against his own good judgment. Yet the man's general demeanor had won him, had made him feel there was no duplicity to fear here.

Was that a characteristic of a successful charlatan? The ability to beguile ingenuous victims into believing that all intentions were innocent? Henry could not say he was not assailed by a doubt or two, but he did not feel threatened, nor did he regret his invitation.

Twelve

Mr. Kimball arrived a little before seven, accompanied by Mr. Amos Fielding. Dinner was pleasant. Mrs. Folsum, Lydia, and Madge had combined to prepare steak and kidney pie with steamed cabbage. Madge served, nervous at first, but confident as the guests proved congenial and pleasant, and courteous enough to make her feel as she were their equal. She wore a carefully starched pinafore with a white ruffle and looked prim and efficient, as indeed she was. Lydia did not hesitate to leave the table and enter the kitchen fray if ever the need should arise. She rendered no loyalty to the stamp of aristocratic distance that her breeding would entail upon her but felt deeply beholden to the efficient operation of her household, and though Madge knew her place, Lydia and Henry had never treated her with less deference than they extended to any other human associate. She always seemed much younger than her actual age, with a figure that could claim no buxomness and limbs still twig-like despite Lydia's assiduous and lengthy campaign to fatten her. But her luminous eyes and her effusive energy belied the image of fragility that her diminutive slenderness suggested.

Oddly, the more voluble of the guests was Mr. Fielding, who chatted freely and laughed readily. Henry expected greater loquacity from Kimball, remembering the air of authority and the easy flow of his sermon. Reverend Preese, who tutored Henry with such arduous care, might have winced at the American's diction from time to time, but Henry could not remember a more engaging delivery. Persuasive. Not the least stylized or pompous. He remembered Kimball's candid, disarming gesture of removing his coat to compensate for the sweltering summer temperature in the warehouse, and more unexpected still, his unabashed invitation for all the coat-wearing men in the congregation to join him. He seemed thoroughly genuine in his concern for their comfort, and no one who heard him would doubt his own conviction regarding the message he delivered. Henry himself did not doubt his sincerity, and he admired the man but not his message. He half expected that he would renew the subject and at closer quarters attempt a conversion. He did not expect this quiet reticence. Kimball appeared pleasant but distant, his manner charming, his smile infectious, but what was missing, besides loquacity, was the glint of irony Henry had noted. Amos Fielding spoke freely of his life in England, his profession as a tradesman, and his conversion to Mormonism. Henry listened politely while Lydia held up the conversational obligation with interest and courtesy. They all laughed and joked together, with only an occasional but always timely quip from Mr. Kimball.

After the meal, they repaired to the withdrawing room while Madge began the clean-up chores. As they sat, Mr. Kimball gazed out the window, as though intent upon something flying in the garden and then dropped his gaze to the floor. When he looked up again, his eyes were alive with the spark of irony Henry had seized upon the day before, though he wondered now if irony was the right word. Now the look was serious, all playfulness aside. What Henry now perceived was a strange ambivalence, an awareness of the present moment while assimilating something from a world beyond time.

"Brother Glendrake, you know why we're here. Thank you both, and little Madge and Mrs. Folsum. The dinner made my home seem much nearer." He smiled slightly, almost imperceptibly, and met Lydia's gaze with friendly understanding. "But I'm concerned for Mrs. Plowhurst—Emmeline—and I must do what

I can to persuade Mr. Plowhurst to release her. That's my responsibility, I believe. Sister Glendrake, I know your concern. A very real concern. I'm not belittling it, not at all; I share it. Yet I feel I must make the attempt to stop this hellish injustice if I can, and if her husband refuses to budge, he must then bear full responsibility for her . . ."

"But . . ." Lydia broke in.

"I know, Sister. Emmeline could suffer for what I feel compelled to do. But I promise you, what I do will bring a swifter resolution than if I ignored the situation." He glanced now in Henry's direction. "I've only met her a few times, but I can tell you, she has a firm grasp upon her faith. She appears quite passive, but that passivity is misleading." He shifted his gaze back to Lydia. "She won't renounce her convictions, and by now she is desperate, with only her faith to cling to. I must give her something more if I can. If I go, she will know I was there for her and she will take courage."

"But she probably won't know! Plowhurst won't let you past his door, and Emmeline's bedroom is removed–quite distant, " Lydia protested, nervously knitting her fingers together.

"She'll know. Of that I'm certain, as I'm certain that I must do this. Will you show me how to get to the Plowhurst place?" He looked resolutely now at both Lydia and Henry. "We should leave as soon as possible tomorrow"

Lydia hesitated. Henry spoke first.

"Of course. I frankly don't know what you expect to accomplish, and personally, I doubt that anything can come of it, but on the other hand, I suppose things can't get much worse for her."

"Thank you, Brother Glendrake. Something will come of it. I can't be specific, but it will be according to God's wisdom, not ours. I wish I could promise you that Emmeline will survive this and have her life and freedom restored without dire consequences. I can't make that promise. But her life is precious, as she is a valiant and courageous soul, beyond anything her friends ever suspected. What develops will be for her eternal good and the good of many." He paused, and walked slowly to the window and fastened his gaze in the distance. "You won't see that immediately perhaps, and some will never acknowledge it, but you will. Her children will remember her courage."

Lydia was weeping quietly, and Madge, listening surreptitiously from behind the door, also wept.

"Can you point me to the Plowhurst house?" Kimball asked, turning back to face them.

"I'll walk with you, take you there," Henry volunteered.

"That will do up to a point. Amos and I will go alone to the door. Or perhaps not. Perhaps I should go alone. I'll think on that as we walk."

Lydia excused herself.

Henry showed the missionaries where they would sleep. They thanked him and bade him goodnight.

Mid-morning the next day, Henry walked between his two guests as they made their way toward the Plowhurst estate. The atmosphere was humid and warm, the hedgerows alive with sparrows and goldfinches, their urgent chirping contrasting with the group's grim and silent contemplations. Henry finally broke the silence:

"Mr. Kimball, forgive my curiosity. Your parishioners—that is, your congregation—call you Brother Kimball, and you return the compliment by doing the same for them."

"Pardon me?"

"I mean you call each other brother and sister."

"Yes."

"Is it a . . . recognition of . . . ah . . . is it a title reserved for faithful converts? I notice you don't do it to everybody—Rupert Plowhurst, for example. You don't hesitate to use the customary titles of polite address, Mr., Mrs., sir, madam—as you did with Lydia and me when we met you."

Now Henry could see again the irony that had captivated him at yesterday's first meeting playing with the phantom of a smile that flitted across Kimball's face as he answered, "It's common among us to recognize our brotherhood."

"Then I feel I should explain that you have misread our intentions. Mine and Lydia's. We have no intention of altering our affiliation or our present loyalties."

"I know that, Brother Henry." Again appeared the fleeting smile that betrayed his awareness of Henry's discomfiture as he used the title. "You have no immediate interest in our doctrine, but your indifference to it has not made you hostile. Even without understanding our position, you welcomed us to your home, extended us hospitality and respect. That makes you a friend, not an enemy. No small blessing for us. A sort of refuge–an island of refuge in a sea of hostility."

"But . . ."

"The fact is, I have fallen into a habit, maybe an embarrassing one for you. *Brother* and *sister* are not official titles among members exclusively but merely a recognition of a simple fact: We are children of the Most High, His spiritually begotten offspring. When I call a man *Brother*, I'm simply acknowledging the paternity that binds us all to God. I fall victim to the practice almost unconsciously on occasion, in company with men I feel compatible with. People I like and respect. Sorry if I blundered. I don't mean to make you uncomfortable."

Henry grinned in spite of himself. "Well, I see that I have sustained no great injury. Rather a compliment, what? No harm done."

Kimball's smile spread. He put his hand lightly on Henry's arm. "Thank you, Brother Henry."

Henry felt strangely warmed by the touch, not in the least invaded.

The group fell silent again as they approached the Plowhurst gate. Kimball broke the silence as he put his hand on the latch.

"I have a feeling I should deal with this alone, as I suggested last evening. Would you both consider taking a stroll together, keeping an eye on my progress?" He chuckled. "You may have to rescue me. Who knows? I doubt this will take too long, though, so don't go far."

Henry nodded. Amos Fielding questioned, "Sure you don't want me to stay with you?"

"Yes, I'm sure. I don't want any neighborly discord to develop between Plowhurst and Brother Glendrake, and I don't want the man to feel we can only face him if we outnumber him. I don't want to create the impression we are ganging up." A hint of flinty resolve colored the slight smile that stole into his expression. "But I especially don't want him to think that I fear him. Let me do this alone."

Henry and Amos walked on, taking a path that led to a hedgerow, where they could watch without being observed from the house. A raven scolded them from a tree near their hiding place. Henry sat on a mound and parted the foliage with a stick and peered through the tangle of leaves and branches to monitor Kimball's venture.

"He needn't have concerned himself over neighborly discord," Henry muttered. "Plowhurst has never wasted what fondness he might feel for his neighbors on me. Besides, I already tried to convince him to act reasonably, but I'd have had a warmer reception from a jilted grizzly bear."

Fielding laughed softly. "You might be amazed at what Heber can do. He might be just the one to make the grizzly dance."

"I've seen that he's persuasive. And he did get past the footman," Henry observed. "I didn't think he'd get that far. He's talking to Plowhurst himself now."

Fielding, resting with his back to the hedgerow, quickly straightened and turned, scurrying to find a clearing that would give him a view of the action. When he finally found a spot, he grumbled:

"Looks disappointing. Can't see a great deal, but the man appears a bit agitated, doesn't he?"

"Not too surprising. The Lord Himself had enemies He couldn't convince, as I remember. Mr. Kimball's probably discovering what it's like to deal with one of those."

Again Amos chuckled. "You may be right, but don't call Heber dead as long as he's still breathing. He doesn't give in easily."

Henry could discern, even from a distance and with the hedge to challenge him, that Kimball's posture was stiff, as though facing a threat, his stout figure erect, his head high and unflinching, and Plowhurst was gesticulating angrily. Then suddenly Plowhurst lunged toward Kimball, taking a step as though to strike. Shouts reached the onlookers. Plowhurst was shrieking unintelligible imprecations. Kimball did not move. Plowhurst stopped short of the threatened mayhem, trembling, almost twitching before Kimball's utter calm, stared in impotent hatred for an instant and then whirled and slammed the door, leaving his antagonist alone and motionless for several seconds. Deliberately, very slowly, Kimball turned and began walking calmly to the gate, opened it, closed it so gently it almost appeared that he feared to break it and then walked on, his step even, measured, tranquil, in the direction he had seen Henry and Amos take as they left him. They immediately abandoned their cover and started toward him.

Heber was somber but otherwise showed no agitation or distress.

"No luck this time, Heber?" Amos asked as soon as they met.

"Not with Mr. Plowhurst. But I know Emmeline heard him. The house is large but not large enough to shield anyone from the noise he made when I told him what I had come for and tried to reason with him. She'll know we were here, and the Lord will comfort her and give her courage."

His promise did little to reassure Henry. Given Rupert's angry disposition, Emmeline, just as Lydia feared and predicted, would bear the brunt of his rage. They returned to Horse Stone House with little further commentary. Lydia met them with both eagerness and dread. She led them to the withdrawing room and bade them sit, and upon hearing the result of their venture, she yielded to the dread. Her chin dropped and her eyes scanned the floor. They all fell silent. At length, Lydia broke the silence. "Something awful is going to happen, I'm sure of it. Mr. Kimball, I wish you hadn't . . ."

Kimball's voice was gentle as he cut across her comment. "Sister Glendrake, I know. Believe me, I know what you're feeling. But I must tell you–How do I explain this? You could take me for a bumptious busybody with holier-than-thou self importance, and it's not that way at all. I wish Brother Joseph were here to do this for me. You know that I did hear you, Sister Glendrake, when you warned me not to intervene as I have." His eyes, so tenderly sympathetic, moistened and held her captive. "I considered what you said, and I prayed for guidance. I prayed a good deal of the night away. I have to follow the feelings of my heart when I pray, because those are the Lord's way of telling us He has heard, and His way of sending an answer. He tells us in our minds and in our hearts. That's the voice I heard."

Neither Lydia nor Henry had anything to say. Kimball drew a long sigh and then continued on. "I also heard it when Mr. Plowhurst slammed his door in my face. I knew then that his anger would overflow and injure the innocent." He lowered his head. "That's the way of all evil impulses, I'm afraid." His head came up again. "But I also understood that what will happen—and it won't be pleasant, I'm sure—will lead to the only solution possible, because Sister Emmeline will not give up her faith and her husband is determined to overrule her; her faith will not yield and his pride will not bend. But something will happen. The only solution acceptable to Emmeline."

He could see Lydia struggling to protest, and he quickly anticipated her. "I know you question how Plowhurst's rage can lead to any kind of happy outcome, and I have to confess I don't know. I can't foresee anything pleasant, as I said, but I trust the Lord, whose ways are to us sometimes mysterious." He shook his head slowly and sighed again. Then he plunged on: "And this is what makes me tremble. How can you trust me to speak for the Lord? Yet I must. It is a part of my commission. You'll be able to see that Emmeline's hardship will end. Plowhurst's cruelty will not prevail."

Lydia no longer cared to answer. She felt drained of protest, empty, beaten. Henry sat next to her, also bereft of comment. The only noise to intrude upon their silence was the sound of birds outside and the muffled shouts and laughter of workers in a distant field. Finally Amos cleared his throat.

"Heber, do you suppose we might pray with these good people?"

"Brother Henry, what do you think?" Kimball asked. "Can we kneel together to ask God's blessings for Emmeline and all the rest of us?"

Henry cast a quick glance at Lydia, who gave a subtle nod, and then spoke. "Mr. Kimball, our Madge has had as big a part in trying to get Emmeline's release as any of us. Could she join us?"

She knew that Madge had seen to the children, leaving them playing in Helen's room upstairs, and now stood listening just outside the withdrawing room, as near the door as possible to listen and learn what she could of Emmeline's bleak circumstances.

"Of course. Bring her in. Mrs. Folsum too, if she's willing."

"Mrs. Folsum went home after dinner. I excused her," Lydia explained as she arose to find Madge, who joined them straightway, shy and trembling. She dutifully knelt with the rest when Brother Kimball invited them to.

His prayer, like the sermon they had heard on Sunday, had such little of formality in it that it sounded like the unrehearsed plea of a distressed son facing a revered parent. The plea laid out all their feelings of pain for Emmeline, her needs that only the Father could supply, their frustration at the intransigent ideology that held her captive. Then Kimball prayed for Rupert Plowhurst, asking for a blessing on him, that his tormented mind could find a measure of peace, that the Holy Spirit might reach and soften his heart. It was an expression of sympathy, and if not full understanding, at least a recognition of in-bred and prevailing social motives for Rupert's stubborn stance. Henry caught, or at least suspected, a note of futility in the request, and confirmed his suspicion when he heard Kimball say, "And if his heart refuses to let thy Spirit in, may our Emmeline find her own way out of her bondage, with her faith to comfort her and her courage to sustain her." Then followed the missionaries' gratitude for the blessings of good friends who did not hesitate to aid men of good will whose creeds did not match their own. Then he became specific: "Bless Brother and Sister Glendrake and little Madge. Bless them for their gentleness, their integrity, their generosity. And bless them with the unfolding understanding of Thy hand in their lives, the dawning of faith in the restoration of Thy kingdom."

After the "amen," Henry felt vaguely uneasy. He did not object to the prayer that included their names, yet he felt uncomfortable with the latent praise for his goodness. He did not feel particularly "good." He was just exercising average yeoman hospitality and human decency, or allowing that there might be value in claims outside his own. But the assumption that faith was dawning in what Kimball regarded as the restoration of God's kingdom troubled him more. A gesture of common courtesy and basic hospitality did not amount to faith in anything.

Kimball stayed on his knees, his thoughts submerged in something quite personal, but Amos Fielding stood, a tacit suggestion that the prayer was over. The rest followed, and finally Kimball himself stood, drawing a contemplative breath, almost a sigh.

"We'll be going now, Brother Henry. It's a fair piece that lies between us and Woodplumpton."

"I'll get the carriage. Drive you into Eccleston."

"No, thank you, Henry," Kimball continued. "It's not that far to Eccleston. The money you gave us on Sunday is sufficient to hire a cab from there."

Henry felt a slight jolt. Kimball had called him by his Christian name, without the formality of a title, even the title of "brother." It was a familiarity that might be interpreted as an affront, a breach of manners. Yet he felt something he welcomed rather than resented.

"But . . ." he began to argue.

"We walk a great deal. It gives us time to let our thoughts ripen, or time to change our opinions, if we need to. Thank you both. Your home is a haven, because there's love here. And thank you, little Madge. You're a fine, energetic young lady, a blessing to this house, and one day you'll have a house of your own to bless."

Madge blushed deeply, confused and embarrassed, finding no response but a rather awkward reverence, something between a bow and a curtsy. The thought of a home of her own loomed as foreign to her as a flight to the moon. She belonged to this house. Kimball smiled at her confusion and took her hand.

"Don't be embarrassed, Madge. The Lord won't forget you. He has already surprised you with a few things you never expected, hasn't He?"

Almost voiceless, she managed, "Yes, sir, 'E 'as." She blushed again at the sound of her own voice.

Kimball turned to Henry and Lydia. "I won't be able to see the end of this, Henry. I had hoped that Plowhurst would show a little flexibility and I could leave assured that Emmeline would . . ."

"Leave?" Lydia asked, almost gasping.

"Yes, I have obligations in London and Preston that I had better mind soon, and they're quite far apart, so I can't put it off any longer. I'm sure you'll be able to look to Emmeline when she is free to . . ."

"But you can't leave. She will be devastated without you here when she . . ." Lydia began.

"You are her friends, the ones she will count on. Amos will stay. Emmeline will be in capable hands."

Henry could not understand the emptiness that invaded him. Kimball continued. "I wish I could stay until something better developed for her. I did what I could, but I certainly didn't heal any wounds. Something will come of it yet."

Again that "something" that would develop soon, something that would release Emmeline, or at least change her situation. A resolution of some sort, but a resolution that, in Kimball's words, might not be pleasant. Henry acknowledged that he was drawn to this man, even felt inclined to trust him, as he would a proven friend. Then his mind lurched back to the question he had asked himself just two days earlier: Is that ability to build instant trust the gift of an accomplished charlatan? Would he continue to trust him, regard him as a friend, or would he curse him for striking up that friendship only to destroy it with some unspeakable religious outrage, some fanatical doctrine that had already sown the seeds of Emmeline's destruction? Was Kimball's concern for Emmeline connected to his knowledge of her commitment to that doctrine, and was it evil, as Emmeline's father had labeled it?

"Sorry to learn you're leaving."

"I'm sorry too. But you'll be equal to whatever happens. Amos will know what to do."

"Mr. Kimball—Heber, I think you realize . . . well, I already explained, but I need you to understand, Lydia and I have no affiliation with your creed, or intention to . . ."

"Yes, I remember, Henry. Don't worry. The Lord knows you better than you know yourself. He knows your heart. You won't fail Him; you will make the right choices for your family. I know you will. You'll have the Lord's blessings, and one day you'll rejoice in His goodness, beyond anything you now know."

A heavy silence followed. Kimball would be leaving, and Henry felt bereft of a cherished friendship, though he had met the man a scant three days earlier. Kimball turned, drawing in a breath, a sigh of resolution. Lydia stood serene, but Henry saw tears welling in her eyes, and a glance at Madge surprised him. Tears streaked her thin face.

Kimball stopped as he and Amos reached the door, and turning again, he asked, "Did Emmeline give you something? Mr. Plowhurst raved about her coming to you with a book."

"Yes," Lydia answered. "She left us her Book of Mormon."

"Hm. Still have it?"

"Yes."

"Read it?"

"Most of it," Lydia confessed. "I put it aside when I became ill, and then all this with Emmeline started and I haven't had time or a tranquil mind for reading." She did not mention Henry's early objections to the enterprise.

Kimball nodded and walked out into what had become a cloudy summer day. Amos smiled and pressed Henry's hand, then took Lydia's for a quick squeeze, then Madge's, muttering his own good-byes, and followed Kimball out, Henry at his heels.

Outside, Henry once more shook hands with the two men, the unusual American preacher and his English convert. Then he watched them walk away, their steps thoughtful but brisk. They clearly meant to lose as little time as possible. They were a considerable distance before Henry, quite suddenly, shouted, "Heber! Amos!"

The two stopped in their tracks and turned in surprise.

"Wait a bit. Come back! I need another word with you," he called. He started walking toward them and they started, hesitantly at first, toward him. When they met, Henry, betraying some excitement, explained, "It suddenly occurred to me that I have business in Eccleston. Rather urgent, actually. If I don't do it now, I will surely have to see to it later. Immediately is none too soon, so wait for me while I fetch the coach. Please allow me to convey you as far as I'm obliged to go for my own needs."

Heber nodded his consent, looking a bit puzzled. Henry called toward his shop, "Hector, would you be so good as to fetch my horse? Take it to the coach. I'll meet you there and help you with the hitching."

Hector dropped his task and did as he was bidden. As they hitched the horse to the coach, Hector asked, "Will you need me to drive for you, sir?"

"No, Hector, I'll drive myself."

"I 'adn't remembered you was goin' to Eccleston today, sir," Hector ventured.

"It wasn't planned, but I do have to go. Something urgent. I'd be grateful if you would continue here while I'm gone and attend to anyone who might be bringing us business."

"I can't quite rid myself of the notion that we're putting you out," Heber said.

"It's just as I told you, Heber," Henry insisted. "My present business is something I must do, and without delay."

He took his place on the driver's seat, his companions behind, and conversation stopped until they reached Eccleston, where Henry once again took reluctant leave of his friends and then turned his horse toward the vicarage.

Temperance met him in the library at the vicarage where the maid who opened for him led him while she summoned her mistress.

"Henry, it's so good to see you. Well, perhaps it's not so

good. You look completely unlike yourself. In fact, you look positively grim."

"I have to speak with Hugh, Temp. Rather urgent, I'm afraid."

"What's the matter?"

"I'll tell you later. For now, just be a good girl and lead me to your husband."

She took him to the garden where Hugh was working and discretely excused herself. Hugh and Henry followed the cordial ritual of friendship and respect, shaking hands, mutually smiling, and muttering the usual greetings. Henry came to the point of his errand.

"Hugh, I know you are acquainted with the Plowhursts. I seem to remember your saying that Rupert was less than pleased with Emmeline's curiosity and interest in the book she lent to Lydia."

"Little wonder, I should think. Mrs. Plowhurst, though I met her only recently and know her quite superficially, did not strike me as flighty and irresponsible, as she now appears to be. Appearances frequently mislead us, what?"

"That's still a hasty charge to lay on her. She is neither flighty nor irresponsible, unless harmless curiosity counts to make her so."

"If indeed it is harmless. I find it difficult to blame Plowhurst for his displeasure. One's religion is hardly a trivial concern."

"Nor is cruelty, insensitivity, and gratuitous harshness. His displeasure! Rupert has refused to listen to his wife's motives, consider her personal needs, or entertain even the scantiest explanation for her actions and has shut her away in her room, depriving her of visits or sociability with anyone; not even her closest friends may see her. She is a prisoner in Plowhurst's house."

Hugh looked shocked, frowning. "Surely it's not . . . hasn't reached such an extreme measure as that?"

"Yes it has! We—Lydia and I—are not welcome there. In my case, I suppose Rupert could always find a pretext for excluding me, but Lydia is quite another matter. I expect he resents her befriending his wife in her sincere desire to find if there's any substance to what the preachers brought her. That's her only trespass,

Hugh, her desire to know, her eagerness to supplant ignorance with understanding! Confound it, man, that's not a criminal Plowhurst has imprisoned!"

Hugh stared at his feet. "Still," he ventured, "she should obey her husband."

"Oh, rubbish, Hugh, would *you*? Could you consent to obey that bully?"

"But a wife must . . ."

"A wife must submit. Doesn't matter what the situation, he must be right and she must follow him. God help us, Hugh. God help us all if we really believe that."

Hugh looked up, meeting Henry's blazing gaze.

"I . . . I will visit the Plowhurst house myself. I'll go this afternoon. I may have no more leverage there than you, but we will see what the vicar can do."

<hr />

Alone with Madge, Lydia questioned, "Madge, did you see Nora last Monday?"

"Yes ma'am. At the market, same as always."

"Did she mention her mistress?"

"Yes ma'am. But that were afore Mr. Kimball came to 'er 'ouse. 'E din't visit until that afternoon. Nora said things was about the same; 'er mistress, Mrs. Plow'urst—she cries some, but stays the same and ain't no worse. She 'opes for more letters fum us, I think."

"Tomorrow is Wednesday. You'll see Nora again, most likely. Just tell her all that has happened, and tell her I will write again next Monday; just have her carry that message to Emmeline."

When Madge returned from the market the next day, she did not mention anything related to her purchases there and dropped them on the kitchen table as she began to speak, eyes wide and serious.

"Mrs. Plow'urst, ma'am. She ain't bein' fed. 'Er 'usband won't allow Nora to bring 'er nuffink and says she'll get food wen she gets smart enough to give up 'er foolish notions. She ain't et since Monday, wen Mr. Kimball went to 'er 'ouse."

"Good heavens! Go get Henry, Madge. He'll be in the barn, of course, and won't welcome you until he knows what it's about."

Madge hurried out, not even minding that Henry had strict rules about interruptions during his working hours, and she scarcely had time to articulate her message. Her pale face and agitated manner spoke before she could get her voice to function, and her first words were enough to confirm his apprehension.

"Mr. Glendrake, sir, the mistress sent me . . ."

Henry dropped his task and ran without hearing more, ran into the house quite prepared to find his wife gasping for air, as had happened before. Lydia, startled to see his ashen face and the near panic in his eyes, gasped, "Henry, what . . . ?"

Just as Henry all but shouting, said, "Lydia, what . . . ?"

Both began talking at once and then finally calmed enough to sort out their separate concerns.

"I'm all right, Henry. It's not my lungs, it's Emmeline. Madge brings word from Nora that Rupert has resolved to starve her until she relents. She hasn't eaten since Mr. Kimball's visit."

"Rupert has . . . Damn him! Damn his miserable, narrow, prejudiced . . ." his voice trailed off into a sputter of fuming indignation. He looked out the window for a minute to collect his thoughts, his hands knotted into fists. He turned back to his wife, who looked pale and questioning. When Henry spoke again, his voice was low and resolute.

"I'll have Hector drive you to the Hamiltons. Tell Howard. He'll listen now. He has to. Emmeline's life is not in danger yet. Two days is merely a discomfort, not a real threat, but that will change. Howard will listen when you tell him she could starve. I'll saddle up and ride to Woodplumpton and speak with Superintendent Pembroke. If Nora will testify, this *is* a matter for the police."

Henry instructed Hector to set aside his assigned workload and prepare the horses and carriage to drive Lydia where she needed to go. Then he saddled his own horse for his journey to Woodplumpton, at least an hour's ride. They worked swiftly, but all the preparations took the better part of an hour before he could get started. Lydia was off in the direction of the Howards' and Henry in the direction of Woodplumpton when he suddenly reigned in his mount and turned, galloping swiftly to catch Lydia's coach.

"Lydia!" he called. She turned.

"Drop by the vicarage. Mention this to Hugh. Tell him all that has happened."

He rode away again.

Thirteen

Emmeline's hunger twisted her insides. Smells from the kitchen invaded her room, smells she had hardly noticed before, except as pleasant harbingers of an impending meal. She coughed. She had been coughing for days, even before Rupert's edict. Her eyes burned. A severe cold had settled deep in her lungs. She coughed again and buried her face in her pillow, hoping to keep out the smell of food. She felt weak, terribly weak. Her muscles and joints ached, her chest burned, and it was worse than the burning in her eyes. She knew the signs of feverishness. Her deprivation had surely not been lengthy enough to cause death. Not yet. But the cough, the mucous, the fever all made her wonder if she were already nearing it.

What did it matter? Perhaps death was her only hope of relief. In life she would always have to deal with Rupert, his malicious intransigence, his churlish service to what he perceived as social legitimacy. God for Rupert had no dynamic presence; He was a vast, static weight, incapable of flexibility or affection, indifferent to changing, evolving human needs, a cosmic presence whose only function was punitive. How delighted Rupert would have been to live in another time, another place. Spain! Three centuries ago, if he were a willing servant of the Inquisition under King Philip II, Rupert would certainly have called it the Holy Office! She remembered vaguely her days, not too long past, as a school girl, remembered learning of the hermetic Spanish king, his pious, and in her view, fanatical dedication to preserving the values of the Mother Church, and saw King Philip as the one most responsible for Spain's obvious decline in prominence. But Rupert would have loved Philip.

Her thoughts made her smile in spite of her pain. Strange that she would even entertain such rambling. Her head ached; the ringing in her ears isolated her, blocked her from the reality of meal preparation and the sounds of her children, but it did not block the smells, nor did hiding her face in her pillow. Does hunger follow us when we die? she wondered. Silly thoughts. Why would one feel hunger without a body to nurture?

Why could she not think of something else, anything else? Food dominated all her awareness now, yet she noted that her pain did not seem associated directly with her need for food. The aching joints and muscles, the burning lungs, the ringing in her ears—these belonged with the fever, the chills, the cough. No matter. It was all one bundle of misery she could not wish away. When her head cleared enough to sort out her thoughts, she prayed. When she did not pray directly, she prayed peripherally. Sometimes she would ask, "God, Father, dear Father, may I not find relief? Please help me, send me strength," and she would feel comforted. But the hunger and the burning would always return, like the cold that invades on winter nights when the fires die. Then a calm settled on her, quite beyond all her other sensations. She still knew she was hungry, still felt the sting in her lungs as she breathed, still felt the throbbing in her ears and the dull ache in her head, the cloying torment in her muscles and joints. But something superceded all of it—a voice she felt but could not hear. She knew, without words to tell her, that she would find deliverance, and she slept, not peacefully, but mercifully.

Nora slipped the key into her pocket, the key entrusted to her by her redoubtable employer, but only after he had assured himself that she carried no food in defiance of his orders and after repeating his threat of dismissal without references. He finished with his typical compassionate lenity: "You have less than an hour to change the mistress's bedclothes and tidy her room. I expect you to finish and leave without dalliance."

He left instructions with the cook that Nora was to have no access to the kitchen in his absence and further directed Fern, the parlor maid, always under the same threat of dismissal, to see that Nora did not smuggle anything into Emmeline's room.

"I'm going into Eccleston; I expect I'll be gone an hour or two. Nora, you are to leave the key with Mrs. Thurman. She expects to receive it in less than an hour, as I have said. Less than an hour. Am I clear, Nora?"

Nora nodded soberly, perhaps sullenly, but without hesitation that would cause him to suspect her of anything but the natural resentment to which he was accustomed.

Satisfied that he had covered all contingencies, Plowhurst nodded to his footman and they made their departure.

Nora stepped softly to Emmeline's room, inserted the key as quietly as possible, and twisted it gently in the lock, hoping not to startle her mistress. As she had hoped, Emmeline was sleeping. She looked about to assure herself that Fern was nowhere close. She knew that none of the help wasted any love on the master, but neither could they afford to defy him. Nora alone dared, and she trembled, knowing that in spite of their sympathy, Fern and Mrs. Thurman would protect themselves.

She walked slowly to Emmeline's bed and bent over her, touching her softly.

"Mrs. Plow'urst, ma'am."

Emmeline awoke with a slight start.

"Nora. Oh, Nora, thank you for . . ."

"Mrs. Plow'urst, we've got ter go."

"Go? Where, Nora? I can't . . ."

"'E's gone fer a bit, ma'am. Whilst 'e's away, we orta go."

"But you can't . . ."

"I can, ma'am. I'll find me way. Ain't nuffink worse than watchin' you starve, and I ain't goin' ter do it. No, ma'am, I ain't."

"Bless you, Nora. I . . . I'm so . . . so weak. I don't know if I . . ."

"We 'ave ter do it, ma'am. Don't 'ave no choosin' of it, as I can see. Whilst 'e's away."

"I need . . . I must take some things . . ."

"There's no time, ma'am! We've got ter go now! 'E gave me scarce a hour, and I'm ter give the key back ter Mrs. Thurman. We can't 'ave nobody see us leave, neither. They don't 'old wiv Mr. Plow'urst's 'ard ways, but they 'ave ter work, and we can't trust 'em, we can't. Not wiv 'im and 'is tellin' 'em they'll be put out wivout no letter."

"But you, Nora! It will happen to you!"

"Can't mind that, ma'am. Mrs. Glendrake will 'elp me there, per'aps. Don't you worry none, I'll find me way, as I said. 'Urry now, please, ma'am!"

Emmeline swung slowly from the bed and stood up. As the blood drained from her head, her vision blurred and she faltered, swaying on her feet. Nora caught her, holding her up.

"Wot's 'appenin', ma'am?"

"Nothing, Nora. It's passing now. I stood up too quickly. There. I can walk now. Where will we go?"

"To the Glendrakes, says I. Don't know as we 'ave no other way ter go. Mrs. Glendrake will 'elp us, I'm sure of it."

"So am I. She will help." Her voice was faint.

"Come, ma'am. We can't wait no more. We 'ave ter go whilst Fern ain't watchin'."

All Emmeline's thoughts seemed to be swirling just out of reach. She had felt reassurance that delivery would come, and Nora was answering the promise, but her movements betrayed her weakness, the ache in her joints and muscles, the ringing in her ears. She tried to answer Nora's urging, but the throbbing in her brain impaired her reflexes. Nora took her arm, pulling her along. They descended the stairs, Nora cautious now, but moving as deftly and silently as she could. Emmeline responded, excitement rising in her despite her weakness. They reached the door.

"It's raining!" Emmeline gasped.

Nora nodded, putting her finger to her lips, imposing silence.

She crept stealthily to the umbrella stand and seized an umbrella. Then she ushered Emmeline out, closing the door without a sound. She hurried through the drenching summer storm, pulling Emmeline along and opening the umbrella as they ran. They were soaked by the time it was of any use to them. Emmeline's cheeks were flushed and her lungs burned. She slowed her steps.

"Can't . . ." she gasped.

Nora put her arm about her waist and practically lifted her along.

"Got ter get outa sight!" she insisted.

Emmeline took a deep, tortured breath and began to run with Nora, matching her step for step until they reached the bend in the path that would shield them from view, then stopped, staggered a few steps and sank to the ground, mud soiling her skirts. Her breath came in great heaving, searing gasps, her vision fading.

"Can't . . ."

She lost consciousness.

Henry returned from Woodplumpton with Inspector Hanning just behind in a hired carriage. His account of Plowhurst's abuse aroused Superintendent Pembroke's indignation, and he lost no time in assigning Inspector Hanning to investigate, with orders to confirm criminal intent and make an arrest if the evidence called for it. Henry's plan was to bypass Horse Stone House and go directly to the Plowhurst farm, but as he neared his house, he saw his team and carriage standing at the door and another carriage just behind it. He identified the second carriage as belonging to Howard Hamilton. He urged his horse to a gallop and turned in.

Lydia met him, anguish in her eyes. "Henry! I'm so glad you're here. Emmeline . . ."

"What?"

"She's here." Her voice broke and tears started. "I sent for Dr. Driscoll. She's going to die, Henry!"

"No, lass, she's not going to die. Two days without food is not enough to kill. How did she . . . ?"

"Nora helped her to get here. Oh, never mind that! I'll tell you later. Just get off and come in. We have to do *something*."

Henry leaped from his horse and followed Lydia inside. Inspector Hanning was just pulling up to the gate.

Emmeline lay on the couch in the parlor, her clothes soiled with mud, her eyes closed, her breathing shallow. Nora and Madge stood by, weeping. Mud caked Nora's shoes and covered her clothes. Dr. Driscoll knelt by Emmeline, listening to her breathing, his fingers on her pulse, while Howard hovered at her head, brushing her face with his fingers, tears welling in the eyes he raised to catch Henry's gaze. "Ah, Henry, Henry, I wish I had heard you, listened when you warned me. Emmeline, my little Emmeline, what have we done to you?" The tears spilled over the edge of his eyelids and rolled down his face.

"Is she . . . she's not . . ." Henry sputtered.

"It's pneumonia, Henry," Lydia explained.

"Not starvation, then?" Henry asked without thinking.

"Starvation?" Dr. Driscoll said, curiosity evident. "Why would you think she was suffering from starvation?" He had answered Lydia's summons quite expecting to be treating her or one of her children. When he was led to Emmeline, seeing her condition, he began at once to address her needs, postponing all other questions. No one had explained Emmeline's circumstances.

Inspector Hanning's knock interrupted them, and Madge tried to dry her eyes as she hurried to the door.

"That'll be Inspector Hanning. He was just behind me as I came in."

"Inspector Hanning? What's his business here?" asked Dr. Driscoll.

"Emmeline's husband, Mr. Rupert Plowhurst, has had my daughter shut away, locked in her bedroom for weeks now. And recently, he began to withhold food." It was Howard Hamilton's bitter voice that proffered the explanation.

"What?' the doctor exploded. "Her symptoms . . ."

"I'm sure your diagnosis is quite correct, Dr. Driscoll," Lydia suggested. "Nora tells me Emmeline has been ailing for several days. Started before she was deprived of food."

"How long has this deprivation been going on?" the doctor demanded.

"Nora?" Lydia simply deferred to the one eye witness. Nora wiped her eyes.

"It's true, sir. 'E wouldn't let me bring 'er no food. Not even water. But I brung 'er water wivout 'im knowin'. A little. It were all I could filch wivout gettin' caught."

"How long, girl? How long was she without food?"

"It were the day afore . . . no, two days afore yesterday."

"Then she's had no food for almost three days? Two and a half, what? And very little water?"

"Yes, sir."

The doctor swore. "Why the . . . How could this go on? Why?"

Howard looked away. Henry cleared his throat.

"I spoke to Superintendent Pedmbroke as soon as I learned that Rupert had . . . um . . . isolated his wife. He explained that the law would not intervene as long as she was in no danger. We learned only this morning that Rupert had resorted to starvation."

"What you haven't explained is why? Was he trying to kill her?"

"That, sir, is exactly why I'm 'ere," Inspector Hanning spoke for the first time. "What was the motive for the starvin' of 'er?"

Henry's mouth looked stubbornly hermetic as he glanced at Howard, and he did not care if his face registered a hint of accusation.

Howard looked down and explained in a low voice, "She had joined a church, quite inappropriately, and Rupert was doing what he thought was best, I suppose, to persuade her to . . ."

"He was trying to starve her to break her faith?" the doctor asked icily.

"We thought he was only trying to get her to be reasonable," Howard muttered. He looked longingly at Emmeline, her pallor deathly, her breath shallow, too shallow, too short. "We didn't know . . . didn't know she was sick. Didn't know . . ."

"Didn't know she wouldn't bend, give in to that kind of bullying?" The doctor was ruthless, and Henry, glad not to be the one to say it, applauded silently. "You didn't know, so you allowed it? Just stood aside and let the aggressive bully have his way. That's called consent, isn't it? Bullying the cowardly way."

Howard paled and did not respond.

"This girl stood up to him. To the death, you'd have to say," the doctor went on. "She won't last the night. Probably won't last another hour. That should leave you quite satisfied. One less heretic in the world."

The doctor's sarcasm scorched Howard so deeply he began to weep in shame and devastation.

Dr. Driscoll knelt by Emmeline's form, placed his stethoscope over her heart, and frowned. "One less," he muttered through his teeth. The loneliness and harshness of this death outraged him. He knew that pneumonia might have killed her even had she had nourishment, but the needless brutality of her deprivation certainly had done nothing to ameliorate her condition. Instead of nurturing and care, she had been administered hunger and rejection.

Lydia fled the room, her face buried in her hands. Nora and Madge followed, weeping openly. Inspector Hanning looked about, quite uncertain where to go, what to do next, quite unsure why he was there.

"Was it . . . um . . . I'm sorry, sir, but if there's been criminal intent . . ."

"There was no criminal intent," Howard said, his voice low with grief and bitterness. "There was criminal neglect. I plead guilty to that. I should have intervened. I had warning enough, didn't I, Henry? You may arrest me, Inspector. I will offer no objection or resistance."

Hanning hesitated.

"Inspector, this man is the girl's father. He's not going to be tried for anything. He merely trusted his son-in-law to be humanly and humanely reasonable, and he misjudged him. Hardly believed that his daughter had married an animal," Henry growled. The words were not uttered in a tone to console, but they were friendlier than Howard could have felt any right to expect, and he turned away to hide his weeping.

Dr. Driscoll sighed. "I'm sorry, Mr. Hamilton, if my sweet disposition has added to your grief. I take no comfort knowing that my opinion has been less than consoling. In fact, I find myself wishing I could discover something soothing to say, but I am still quite disturbed that this poor lady was obliged to stand against practically everyone she knew and die alone."

"Not everyone, sir. Henry and Lydia tried. They did not abandon her. They tried to make us see..."

The doctor turned to Henry.

"I'm curious, Mr. Glendrake. Are you a believer?"

"A believer in what, sir?"

"In God."

"Of course."

"You have just exploded a perfectly plausible theory, conceived of careful observation and well-earned cynicism. I counted on sharing it with a fellow atheist, and you have wrecked my expectation. Do you share the same faith as this girl?"

Henry shook his head. "No. But I find no harm in what she professed."

"Ah, but it's not orthodox, is it?" the doctor said archly.

"I know too little to say, Doctor. But I knew Emmeline, and she was incapable of..."

"Curse the day she met those American preachers!" Howard hissed.

"I'm not a religious man, as I have already confessed," the doctor said. "Why should this poor girl be any less entitled to her opinion than you are to yours, sir? Why, if one must believe in God, may not one believe as he or she feels inclined?"

"Because... I don't know. I didn't..."

"Didn't what?"

"Didn't know a great deal about it. Didn't care to. I just wish they had tended to their own affairs and left poor Emmeline alone."

137

"Mr. Hamilton," Henry interrupted. Howard said nothing, but looked questioningly at Henry. "Emmeline died for her belief, whatever it was. I wonder if mine could command such loyalty?"

Hamilton's answer was another flood of weeping.

A loud knock suddenly rattled the front door. Knowing that Madge was indisposed, Henry excused himself to answer it. He hid his surprise when on opening it he met Rupert Plowhurst wearing an expression of almost rabid ire.

"Glendrake..."

"Ah, Rupert. Please come in. Your presence will save someone a great deal of trouble."

"No, I won't come in. I will wait here until you deliver my wife and her dim-witted maid. I expect you..."

"Suit yourself, Rupert," Henry said pleasantly, and shut the door.

Inspector Hanning, hearing from the parlor, came sputtering out.

"Don't let 'im go! 'E's got a lot of questions 'e needs to answer."

"No need to fret, Inspector. He'll knock again."

And the door shuddered under the knock that thundered against it. The circumstances provided little to smile about, but Henry could not suppress a satisfied smirk, and Hanning heaved a relieved sigh. Henry opened the door again.

"Do come in, Mr. Plowhurst," he repeated in a sugary voice, the formality of the renewed invitation as foreign as it was sarcastic.

Plowhurst glowered. If he noticed Hanning standing there, he gave no indication.

"All right, Glendrake, have your fun. I intend to bring charges for this. You are holding my wife here, I know it. Both Mrs. Thurman and our parlor maid are quite sure Nora was bringing her here."

"Why, Rupert? Why did she have to flee your house? From what did Nora think she had to rescue your wife?"

"That's hardly your concern. I demand that you return both my wife and her maid, or I shall take steps..."

"I think I've 'eard enough, Mr. Glendrake," Inspector Hanning growled.

Plowhurst snapped his attention to the inspector, his expression venomous.

"You, sir, have nothing to say in this matter. My business is in regard to my wife and my variance with Glendrake."

"And my business, sir, is the law. You'll 'ave your opportunity with an inquest and the judge, but..."

"What is this fool blathering about?"

"Probably about how you're going to explain yourself in the matter of Emmeline's death. She *is* dead, Rupert." Henry's tone carried no semblance of equivocation.

For a moment, rage struggled with shock in Plowhurst's face. He opened his mouth to shout some imprecation, but the grimness in the expressions of both men cut across his words, and he closed his mouth and swallowed, his face pale; then in a voice low, labored and rasping in his throat, he managed: "I demand an explanation for this outrage. I demand..."

Henry answered evenly, half-smiling. "Don't trouble yourself to adopt airs of indignation and injury, Rupert. There's no way you can turn your despicable cowardice into anything virtuous."

Plowhurst's face turned crimson and he clenched his fists. Henry continued unperturbed. "You have bullied Emmeline from the day you married her, and when she showed herself superior to anything you are or ever have been, or could be, you killed her. In my view, sir, you are a murderer, no matter what might be decided at the inquest."

Plowhurst's eyes dilated in rage and fear.

"Oh, yes, there will be an inquest. You will have your chance to defend yourself, even though in my view you have no defense."

Plowhurst's mouth was working, but no words came. His eyes burned now with hatred, confusion, and the same lingering fear. Henry's voice rolled on, evenly, matter-of-factly: "I find myself hoping that you will carry out the desire I see in your face to attack me. Go ahead, Rupert. Please try. Raise a finger, utter a threat, look menacingly once more in my direction. Almost anything will do, and I shall lay you flat."

Plowhurst fairly choked on his fury and actually took a step toward Henry, who simply smiled and crouched, fully prepared for the onslaught. Hanning moved quickly, placing his considerable bulk between the two.

"No need for that, now. I'll take care of Mr. Plow'urst, and I expect to take 'im in without no injuries to speak of. Yer comin' with me, sir," he said.

Plowhurst found his voice. "I'll do no such thing. I demand to know why I'm being subjected to this vile accusation!"

"There'll be no demandin' from you, sir. Wot there'll be is, you will go quietly with me to the carriage as is waitin' for us, and you'll wait in gaol for the inquest, which is where you'll be 'eard by the judge to see if you'll go to trial. Do your demandin' there, sir, not 'ere."

What Hanning had learned of the girl who died in the Glendrake parlor had not disposed him to look kindly upon the perpetrator of her misery, and though he may have questioned whether Plowhurst was legally liable for her death, he was determined to see that he encounter as much inconvenience as the law would impose, even if it were only the inconvenience of having to seek counsel for his defense. Inquests and trials were public events, and all the details were fodder for reporters and gossips. Even a verdict of technical innocence could leave one socially broken, and Hanning did not doubt that Plowhurst's zeal in imposing his accepted religious practice on his wife stemmed from a vivid social consciousness. The society this man worshiped could create its own hell.

Henry stood still for a few minutes, watching Hanning's skilled persistence and persuasive muscle convince Plowhurst that resistance was both futile and uncomfortable. Then he returned to the parlor where Howard sat with his head buried in his hands while Dr. Driscoll seemed to be pondering out loud: "I have never understood the divisiveness of religion. Seems to create more war than money, poverty, infidelity, or even politics. On the one hand, Christianity preaches brotherhood, compassion, forbearance, and love, but grows thoroughly intolerant and quite contentious in the face of challenging views. I find it more comfortable to question the need to believe in God."

"I forgot all I ever knew of compassion when I allowed that man to mistreat my little girl," Howard said. "What kind of Christian does that to his own child? Or his wife?"

"I'm afraid now is the time for other considerations, Mr. Hamilton," Henry suggested softly. "With Emmeline gone and Rupert detained, we must think of the two children."

"They will come to us," Howard said with quick finality.

"Henry, do you mind if I thrust my spoon into this soup?" Dr. Driscoll ventured.

"Your spoon is as clean as mine for stirring in it," Henry answered.

"As a doctor, I've no small experience with courts, judges, lawyers, all that litigation implies. I've been considering the circumstances of this tragedy, and I have a couple of suggestions."

"I think by now I will not reject out-of-hand any serious suggestion. The last time I did that I lost my daughter," Howard said bitterly.

"Let's move cautiously. There will be an inquest, given the complications of Emmeline's death. I will have to testify that she did not die of starvation. It's impossible to say if her food deprivation even contributed to her death. It did nothing to reassure her or strengthen her system to fight off the invading infection, but she died of pneumonia, not malnutrition."

"But he *was* starving her!" Howard answered hotly.

"Yes, I know. But the infection killed her. That's what the judge will be forced to recognize, and I must give my testimony as to the actual cause, and contributing causes will be suggested but can never be proven, since starvation does not obtain within just two-and-a-half days. So Plowhurst will eventually go free."

"Then. . ."

"Then we need to strike a bargain with him."

"Bargain? I'd sooner bargain with a nervous cobra!" Howard sputtered.

"Just sit calmly until I explain myself, sir. You'll need to let me finish or you won't know what my suggestion consists of."

Hamilton frowned. "All right, I'll listen, but I hope it gets better than I've heard so far."

"Plowhurst will not be convicted, but if all the facts are aired, as I'm sure they will be, his perfidy will become public, and though he won't hang for it, he may suffer disgrace and possibly ostracism."

"That's not a whit, not a mite, not a shadow of what he deserves!"

"That may be; in fact, I agree with you, but it's probably beside the real point. These are facts we will have to face in a British court of law: Rupert Plowhurst did, with excessive zeal and no little cruelty, I'll grant, what any man expects to do in our country. He holds rights and responsibilities, votes for his wife, is legally and financially responsible for her, and traditionally determines the religion his family will practice."

Henry remembered Superintendent Pembroke's almost identical litany designed to excuse the law from intervention. The doctor continued:

"He also determines the wife's social status and may be expected to exercise some measure of firmness if his wife deviates. With Nora's testimony, Henry's and Lydia's, perhaps Madge's, and yours, Mr. Hamilton, we may show criminal intent, but remember that Emmeline defied him, joined a sect that would diminish him—embarrass him, a strange sect quite alien to the orthodox faith she was expected to follow. It's true, Plowhurst will suffer public outrage for trying to starve her into submission, but my testimony of the real cause of death will surely mitigate that outrage."

"What are you saying, man? Are you trying to tell me I must let my grandchildren be raised by that miserable worm, the man who was willing to murder their mother?"

"Before you let your indignation capsize you, sir, remember that you yourself allowed Plowhurst . . ."

"I know that! To my utter shame, I know it! But I didn't know he was capable of starving her!"

"But you must see, given your own view regarding her deviation from traditional practice, how difficult it will be to get a conviction for a death he did not cause. She had been deprived of food for a little more than two days. It no doubt weakened her but did not kill her. They will ultimately excuse Plowhurst. A short jail term, perhaps. But we may have enough, nevertheless."

"Enough for what?" Henry asked.

"Enough to make him malleable, amenable to what I am proposing," the doctor said.

"I've heard no proposal," Howard growled. "All I've heard is that Rupert will likely walk away from this virtually unscathed."

"Not exactly. From what I gather, he is more than mildly sensitive to public opinion. There's still the threat of ridicule, a possible jail sentence, and the problem of what will happen to his children. I don't suggest that either of you should approach him, especially not Henry. Mr. Hamilton, has your relationship with him before this shameful moment been reasonably cordial?"

"Before this . . . Yes, I suppose so. The fact that I did not have the courage to oppose him might suggest that our relations were not acrimonious, but that will never be so again."

"I understand. But you did not face him just now, and that is fortunate. Perhaps he does not even know that you were here. He never got as far as the parlor where Emmeline lay, and I see that as a distinct advantage. You have suffered severely but have not attacked him."

"No, I have not. But rest assured, I will never forego the privilege should it ever come my way."

"Quite. Therefore, I will be the one to speak with him, since I have not suffered outrage at his hand, at least not that touched me intimately as it has you; nor have I offered to 'lay him flat,' as you did Henry."

"I would gladly . . ."

"Oh, yes, I believe you would have, and I confess, I was—well, we all—were a bit disappointed when Hanning intervened. But my point is, you have no leverage with the man, not even if you apologized, which I would never expect you to do. I'm a relative stranger, and my suggestion will be that he avoid all the humiliation of the inquest and trial."

"How?" thundered Howard.

"He can avoid it if we bring no charges or offer no testimony against him. In exchange for that, he will sign a release, placing his children in your custody, yours and your wife's, Mr. Hamilton."

"But then . . . You're asking me to heap even more shame upon myself. May I not ever have the privilege of exposing this man for what he is? Have I not a moral obligation?"

"Mr. Hamilton," Henry said quietly. "The doctor has already explained that we may not expect retribution, or at least very little, through the courts. I believe our first concern should be the welfare of the little ones, and you yourself have already bewailed the possibility that they might have to spend the rest of their lives in Rupert's care."

Howard opened his mouth to interrupt, but Henry hurried on. "If Dr. Driscoll can secure legal release, Rupert's freedom will be a small price to pay. Let God and society take charge of his punishment, and give the children the blessing of a mother they can revere and a father who technically has no blackened name, however much he might have earned it."

Howard dropped his head. "That will give you and Mrs. Hamilton the privilege of their care and teaching, and they will learn pride in their heritage and values they could not acquire anywhere else." Henry continued. A new thought changed his expression. "Mr. Hamilton, I believe it's advisable that you get help from my brother-in-law, Hugh Morecroft."

"The vicar?"

"Yes."

"But surely, he . . ."

"I think he will not countenance Plowhurst's actions. I believe he will see his perfidy and will be our ally, and I believe he will offer able testimony to facilitate Dr. Driscoll's plan."

"But surely he looks darkly upon Emmeline's break with his . . ."

"That may be true, but I'm willing to trust his ability to judge with fairness rather than bias. Just explain everything. Leave out nothing, not even your own dismay at Emmeline's deviation from her original religious moorings."

"Shouldn't you do better at this than I, Henry?"

"No. The vicar sees quite enough of me. He will do better hearing from Emmeline's own father."

"If we may count on his corroboration, or even just make Plowhurst think we have it, our position with him will be greatly strengthened," Dr. Driscoll noted. "It's surely worth pursuing."

Hamilton nodded slowly.

"I shall go to the jail prepared with documents as quickly as possible—tomorrow, if we can arrange it that soon," the doctor continued. "I am not unfamiliar with certain legal manipulators–they resent my calling them that–solicitors. One in particular is a friend of mine. One of my patients, in fact. That's why he is obliged to tolerate my cheek. He will draw up the documents, and I shall present them to Plowhurst, preferably before he recovers from the shock of his arrest."

Howard sat absorbed in the contemplation of Emmeline's serene pallor. A wave of anguish washed through him as he remembered that his wife knew nothing of Emmeline's death, and he would be obliged to tell her. He touched Emmeline's tousled hair and longed to speak to her, ask her what he should do. He saw no torment in the face he gazed on now, only peace. Perhaps that was the answer he needed.

"Do it," he whispered. "Do it, sir."

Fourteen

Dr. Driscoll adroitly managed his "legal manipulator," whose presence quite awed Rupert Plowhurst with an air of legal prescience and the veiled foreboding in his explanation of the likely outcome should there be a public airing of Plowhurst's cruelty. A subsequent visit from Hugh Morecroft, who quite firmly assured Rupert that he would give testimony of Rupert's intransigence as a possible contributing cause of Emmeline's death, strengthened all that the solicitor had already suggested. When Rupert tried to win the vicar's favor by insinuating that all he intended was to bring Emmeline back to the fold, he was met with a very stern and implacable rejection.

"Such cruel measures of persuasion have no place, absolutely no place, in the doctrines of Christianity," Hugh said grimly. "You can never excuse the means you used by appealing to the nobility of your cause. Besides, your cause was clearly not as noble as you would like to make it. It was selfish bigotry, not piety, that moved you, sir."

Legal and social retribution threatened ominously, and nurturing no inclination for nursery duties, Plowhurst found the solicitor's persuasive proposal not merely attractive but imperative. Emmeline's death had caught him by surprise and filed the teeth of his belligerence. Howard and Mrs. Hamilton, though not entirely delivered of their bitterness, felt a rush of relief, having expected resistance or complete recalcitrance. Unaware of the full extent of Dr. Driscoll's skillful orchestration, they were surprised when Rupert even agreed to remain in custody until all the details of the agreement were in place.

Emmeline's two girls adjusted quickly to their new circumstances, sleeping in the same room where their mother had slept, exploring the same corners she had loved. They grieved her loss, of course, but with the resilience of children, they came to bask in the coddling vigilance of their grandparents, whose recollection of omissions made with their daughter whetted their attentiveness toward her children. They spoke often and affectionately of Emmeline, kept her memory before them, showed them their few but cherished photographs, at first avoiding any mention of the cause of her death. Later, when the girls demanded greater understanding, the Hamiltons did not hesitate to affirm that she had died courageously defending her belief in God and her right to worship Him as she chose. They still avoided details, and they never mentioned Rupert. Apparently, the fear of exposing his perfidy kept him at bay, for he never attempted to communicate with his daughters and avoided all association with the Hamiltons. He also turned aside whenever Henry happened in his vicinity. Henry and Lydia saw the Plowhurst girls often, their children already comfortably acquainted.

Nora never returned to the Plowhurst premises. For the present, Henry and Lydia made a place for her at Horse Stone where she shared quarters with Madge. When Henry dropped by the Plowhurst household to retrieve the few belongings Nora had left behind, Plowhurst did not receive him, but Henry made it plain to the footman who did that he would tolerate no excuses or alibis, and that recalcitrance would occasion legal intervention; he said he would return the next day, giving Plowhurst time to collect everything appropriate. As he expected, Nora's belongings were bundled and waiting for him when he returned.

For a few brief days, Nora and Madge combined to attack household chores, giving Lydia more free time than she had enjoyed since her wedding, but she understood that family finances would probably not withstand another monthly salary. Remembering again her mother's household with its small army of servants, she was sure another recruit, more or less, would make little difference to the Smirthwaites. With so many in service, changes were frequent, and Nora, at Lydia's instigation, stepped in to fill a gap when one developed in the Smirthwaite retinue, and with a few minor adjustments, found herself quite content, far more content than ever she had been under Rupert Plowhurst's roof. She always remembered Emmeline's gentleness and missed her sorely, but with her gone, the thought of Rupert's overweening supervision and harsh command made her new position seem a refuge, notwithstanding her challenges as a newcomer among established personnel. Madge had become her dearest friend, and they still saw each other on market days and whenever Nora could get time off for a visit.

<hr />

Early of a Friday morning, Henry finished breakfast and hugged Lydia.

"Don't expect me for supper. I'm staying until I finish me job in Wrightington. I've already spent two full working days there, and I'd like to finish before the weekend, so I'm taking Hector with me. Between us, I think we can do it, but it will be a very long day."

"Shall I not keep something hot for you?"

"No, we'll stop at the pie-maker's in Wrightington. He's always there on the street until very late, unless he manages to sell all his pies. I've never had one, but they look very good."

"You can't work all day without nourishment. I'll pack something for you."

"No, I can't afford the time. Besides, I'm working for Squire Murdock. His footman always brings us something at about midday. That will keep us 'til we meet the pie man."

Lydia nodded and Henry left.

In the evening, after reading time with the children, Lydia and Madge bedded them down and retired to the parlor, where they often went to relax after a day's surprises and routine demands. Neither ever abandoned her position or felt tempted to, though their familiarity would have scandalized most of Lydia's acquaintances, but the great distance between them had grown less with the years, and they had simply come to enjoy each other's company and look forward to quiet time together in the parlor when they could manage it.

Madge looked a bit nervous and started to speak a time or two, seemed to change her mind, and then finally plunged.

"Ma'am?"

"Yes, Madge?"

"Mr. Kimball, um, axed you if you 'ad somfink. It were a book, weren't it?"

"I still have Emmeline's Book of Mormon. That's what he meant. I don't plan to give it to Rupert Plowhurst, though it's legally his. I'm keeping it."

Madge smiled, amused at the thought of Plowhurst's interest in receiving the Book of Mormon. She hesitated before asking, "'Ave you finished wiv it, ma'am?"

Lydia looked up, surprised. "Finished with it?"

"Readin' it, ma'am. 'Ave you read it all?"

"No. Well, almost. I lack a little, but haven't got back to it. With all the—you know, Emmeline's problems . . . I was reading it and when she—wasn't here any more, I didn't . . . Why do you ask?"

"Um, can I read it? Is it too 'ard for me as ain't read very much?"

"No, I don't think so. I know you read the Bible."

"Yes, ma'am. Not fast, I don't, but I reads it and understands wot I reads, mostly. Some words is 'ard, them as I ain't never 'eard."

"I don't think the Book of Mormon is any harder. Maybe a little easier."

"If I shou'nt read it, I won't. If it ain't sinful or sumfink."

"Why would you think that?"

"Because . . . Well, Mr. Plow'urst said . . ."

"Surely you don't worry about what Rupert Plowhurst might think."

"No, ma'am, but we . . . I mean you and Mr. Glendrake ain't gone back to Mrs. Plow'urst's church or nuffin', and Mr. Glendrake won't read it, and you ain't finished it, and I thought maybe I shou'nt be readin' it."

"The truth is, I've had it on my mind. I want to finish it. I'm glad you brought it up." She cocked her head as though struck by a new idea. "I'll go get it!"

She moved quickly to her bedroom where she had left the book unopened on the small table near her side of the bed. It was time to finish the few pages she had not read, and the thought that her reading would scandalize the likes of Rupert Plowhurst made the adventure all the more alluring. No matter that those scandalized would never know; what mattered was that they would disapprove, and she would delight in telling them should they ask.

She returned to the parlor where Madge waited.

"Let's start at the beginning again; that way, you can review what we have covered and it will give you a chance to test your reading. You can go beyond as far as you'd like. Will that do?"

"Yes, ma'am."

They read aloud for over an hour and were still reading when Henry returned from work. From the withdrawing room where he normally lingered, he heard Lydia's voice and recognized that the rhythm was not the rhythm of dialogue. He leaned against the mantle and filled his pipe, not eager to interrupt. Lydia hesitated.

"Henry, are you home?"

"Yes, my dear."

"Hungry?"

"No. We stopped for a pie, as I said we would. Very tasty. Um, go on with your reading, lass."

"We've been at it for quite a while. I'll finish this chapter and stop. It's past time for bed."

Returning to the text, she repeated the last sentence she had read and continued on. Henry sat and smoked before the fire. When Lydia finished the chapter, she shut the book, quietly said goodnight to Madge, and walked softly to her bedroom to wait for Henry. Madge went silently to her own. When Henry joined

Lydia, they did their devotional Bible reading before they blew out the candles.

"Nice of you to read to Madge like that," Henry suggested.

"She wanted it. Her own reading is going well, but reading aloud will help her, and she's very curious about the Book of Mormon."

"Is she? Well, then, you should see that she gets satisfied. Very well done, my dear."

Thereafter, Lydia and Madge made a ritual of the evening hours, bedding the little ones and reading aloud, and frequently Henry listened, smoking his pipe in the withdrawing room. During the day, whenever Madge found a free moment, she read to herself, learning, gaining speed and confidence, re-reading and plunging ahead, so that when evening came, she was often already familiar with the text, but she had not yet found the courage to take a turn at reading aloud for Lydia, preferring just to listen.

During one of their sessions together, Lydia read the line, "Man is that he might have joy." Madge caught her breath.

"I read that meself just this mornin'," she said. "Din't know as how a man was more joyful than a woman."

Lydia smiled and explained that the word *man* was sometimes used to designate all of humankind. The explanation troubled Madge, but when Lydia did not seem inclined to linger on the topic, she asked another question.

"I reads words as I don't rightly understand. Wot *is* joy, ma'am?"

"A happy feeling, Madge."

"Like when you laugh?"

"Well, yes, I suppose. Mm. No. Not that. I think laughter is wonderful, like a release of tension, and it's fun. But it can be wicked too, can't it?"

"Yes, ma'am."

"Fun can be evil. Glee, pleasure, delight—all these can have an evil side. One can take pleasure in another's suffering. Some people seem to take delight in teasing. Sadists may be gleeful when they can cause someone's discomfort."

"Wot's a sadist, ma'am?"

"Oh, it's not important. Let's not worry about it. Perhaps you may never meet one, and I hope you don't. But joy—to me, joy is only possible as a spiritual gift, a confirmation from God, I guess. Oh, I don't know. It's a feeling like—like one I remember when I was a little girl. My father took my sister and me to a show in Eccleston. A group of itinerant players . . ."

"Wot's that, ma'am?"

"Itinerant players?"

"Yes, ma'am. Wot is they?"

"Well, they're actors that go from town to town, setting up a stage, usually in the town square, where they do shows. Acts. You know . . ."

Madge's expression betrayed her perplexity.

"You . . . you never saw one, did you, dear?" Lydia said quietly.

"No, ma'am."

"I'll be sure to take you sometime. Anyway, we went that day to see the show, and we thought it was wonderful. But what I loved most was a little girl, just my age. The daughter of the troupe's director and his wife, who was the principal actress. The girl's name was Roseanne."

"Roseanne?"

"Yes. Before the show began, she found us, Catherine and me, and whisked me off to meet her mother. Catherine didn't go with us; I don't remember why, and I got into trouble with my father for running off without permission. He forgave us, though, and when he met Roseanne's mother after the show, he was so charmed he forgot all about my mischief."

Madge giggled. Lydia paused, and Madge's expression begged for more.

"I never had anyone reach me like Roseanne. She was my friend, instantly. It was as though I had known and loved her forever. And you know something else?"

Madge shook her head solemnly.

"She pulled me out of a much thornier problem. Besides running off without permission, that morning I had put on a bracelet my grandmother had given me. I didn't have permission for that, either. It was supposed to remain in our family safe until I was older, at least eighteen, and I had sneaked it out. I lost it; I never knew how nor where. By the time I discovered I had lost it, it was dark and we were on our way home. It was not practical to turn back. When I told my father, he was not unkind, but he was very displeased."

"'E din't whip yer?"

Again Lydia smiled. "Have you ever seen Henry strike Helen? Or Forest?"

"No, ma'am."

"My father would never have whipped me, any more than Henry would strike one of his children. But he made me confess everything to my mother the following morning. And she was livid!"

"Wot?"

"Uh, very angry. She sent me to my room and made me stay there until she herself released me. My father started back to Eccleston to see what he could do to recover the bracelet, but he met the Withers' carriage . . ."

"Who?"

"The Withers. Oh, I didn't tell you. That's Roseanne's parents. Her name was Roseanne Withers. They were on the road toward our house to return the bracelet, a very costly bracelet, with large emeralds and many diamonds. I apparently had left it in their caravan."

Madge squealed with delight. "She brung it back for you!"

"Yes. I escaped from my confinement—my punishment—and went with Catherine to meet their caravan. When Roseanne got out and started running toward me, holding the bracelet, reaching it out to me, I completely dismissed the gift, the bracelet she had found for me. It was Roseanne herself, my friend, that I cared about. I was—well, I think that's what joy is. I was so full of emotion—so joyous—I couldn't laugh. It was too deep and wonderful for laughter. I wept."

"Cried?" Madge whispered.

"Yes. I cried. I was unspeakably happy."

Madge blinked and nodded.

"I was reading the Book of Mormon myself yesterday," Lydia continued. "I read that Jesus was resurrected, as we read in the Bible, and went to America to visit the people there."

"'E went to America?"

"That's what it says." Lydia thumbed through the pages to locate the passage she wanted to share. Finding it, she began reading: "'And . . . Jesus spake unto them, and bade them arise. And they arose from the earth, and he said unto them: Blessed are ye because of your faith. And now, behold, my joy is full. And when he had said these words, he wept . . .' He cried, Madge. Joy is too deep for laughter." She fell silent, and Madge too was quiet, her eyes moist.

Then, in a breathy whisper, Madge said, "Thank you, ma'am."

"Want to read on a bit?"

Madge nodded, and the reading continued until Lydia caught Madge in a yawn. She smiled and closed the book.

"We'll finish tomorrow night," she said, touching her lightly on the arm, an affectionate gesture of leave-taking as she rose to speak with Henry, expecting Madge to find her way to her bed.

Several days later, on an evening after Henry had spent most of the day in Eccleston, he came to dinner solemnly, with little to say, ate, and then excused himself and went to the barn. Lydia noticed his unusual reticence but quite untypically made no remark. When the children were fed and bedded, Lydia and Madge renewed their nightly ritual, and shortly they heard Henry come in again and settle himself in the withdrawing room. They soon caught the familiar odor of his tobacco, and Lydia assumed that all was normal and his earlier reserve a fleeting mood. She finished a chapter and consulted the clock.

"A bit late. Best put yourself to bed, dear."

Madge nodded and excused herself. Lydia drifted quietly into the withdrawing room where she found her husband scowling slightly in concentration, reading a book with a familiar black binding. He looked up half apologetically.

"I thought I might read a little faster on my own," he said.

"Where . . ."

"Where did I get it? In Eccleston. Went to visit Amos Fielding. He seemed rather pleased to provide me with a copy." He dropped his eyes back to the page.

Lydia smiled at his wry understatement but said nothing. Then the smile blossomed into a low laugh. Henry glanced up again without humor, even with some annoyance. Lydia's laughter exploded like crashing glass and echoed through the house. The sound brought Madge in with tentative step to investigate. She stood in the doorway, hardly daring to hazard an interpretation for what she saw. Henry was sitting stiffly in his chair, his face a mask of grave disapproval and defensive sternness. Lydia, now almost fighting for breath, finally drew in enough air to keep the wave of laughter rolling and reverberating against the walls. Her knees gave way, and she sank to the floor, her face flushed and tears oozing from eyes crinkled shut with uncontrolled mirth. Poor Madge began first to question her mistress's sanity, but straightway modified the thought because in her mind, Lydia's sanity was beyond question, and so she began to doubt her own. Such a scene had never been enacted in this household since she became a part of it, or anywhere else that she could remember. Henry seemed quite determined not to dignify his wife's abandon with any recognition until he saw poor Madge's utter perplexity. Her face looked so pitifully stricken, her eyes so woefully full of question that Henry too began to chuckle in spite of himself, and the hedge he had built to protect his offended dignity crumbled like a clay wall before an avalanche. When Madge finally realized that the tragedy she suspected was a farce to enjoy, she began to cry in sheer relief. Lydia wiped her eyes, and she jumped to her feet still trembling and weak, though her spasms of hilarity died as suddenly as she saw that Madge was crying.

"Madge, what is it, dear?" She hugged her as she spoke.

"I'm sure she thought you had lost all semblance of sanity," Henry mused. "Actually, you have me wondering as well."

"Ain't nuffink, ma'am," Madge sputtered, smiling now, although her face was still lined with tiny rivulets and her nose ran.

"I'm sorry, Madge. Henry looked so . . . so . . ." she began to laugh again. "He tried to make it so . . ." laughter . . . "so natural—

solemn as a druid priest and as natural as a flying cow." Her laughter would not stop.

By now, Madge was laughing too. Henry cleared his throat.

"Madge was quite right, Mrs. Glendrake. You have lost your reason."

He arose with immense dignity, his expression as lively as a dried prune. He tucked the book under his arm and marched to his bedroom without a backward glance, resolute as the commander of a death brigade.

Lydia and Madge were chortling near collapse in each other's arms.

Fifteen

Henry made no mention of the riotous breach of decorum that might have scandalized the neighbors had they witnessed it, but he smiled less than usual. Lydia did not complain, because he appeared more pensive than irritable. Often he was working during their reading sessions, but some weeks after Lydia caught him reading the Book of Mormon on his own, he came in earlier than usual, interrupting their exercises.

"Mind if I join you?" he asked without a shred of diffidence, as though there were nothing unusual in his changed attitude.

Lydia smiled broadly and Madge squeaked with pleasure.

"We're delighted," Lydia said simply. "Madge has read ahead since last evening, and now she's going to read aloud those pages."

Madge blushed and appeared about to decline.

"She's reading very well. You'll be proud of her," Lydia assured.

Indeed, her progress was quite remarkable. When she finished, Lydia encouraged her to continue on, venturing into unfamiliar territory. She complied, and her success confirmed her growing ability, but with Henry present, she began to lose confidence and grew self-conscious. Lydia rescued her then, finishing the chapter. She looked at Henry a little impishly.

"We've each had a turn. Now it's yours. Want to read the next chapter? It's not very long."

Henry did not demure. "Of course," he said dryly.

He read with the same voice Lydia heard each night during Bible reading, his "devotional" voice, without mockery or derision. After he finished, he closed the book and waited silently, expecting Lydia to proffer a quip or witticism. None came. Finally, Lydia sighed.

"It's time for bed, isn't it?"

Madge sat contented and serene in her silence but rose and dismissed herself with a little smile and a nod. Lydia lit a candle, put out the gas light, and took Henry's arm.

"We've had our nightly devotional reading, haven't we?" Henry asked as they walked together to the bedroom.

"Yes, but you could still read from the Bible."

Henry nodded.

A few nights later, Henry again joined them in the now-expected evening exercises, and again he was the last one to read. And once more, they sat in silence when the reading ended. This time, Henry broke the silence.

"I have read all this. I finished the book."

"So did I," Lydia said.

"I don't read as fast as that," Madge apologized.

"You started after I did," Lydia reassured. "Besides, you haven't had the advantage of our years of practice. You don't lack much."

"I doubt that you have to finish the book to know your mind," Henry said. "You already believe it, don't you?"

"Yes, sir," Madge answered.

Henry drew a long breath. "I've been reading every chance I got. I had to know . . ."

"Know what, Henry?" Lydia asked.

"I had to know what gave Emmeline the courage to hold out against Rupert without any help from anyone but you, Lydia."

"Me? I gave her no help at all," Lydia protested. "I even refused her request to read, the help she specifically asked for."

"But you revised your position and you did give her what she asked, and she turned to you, as she knew she could, and came to you for refuge when Nora managed to spring her free. You were her only ally, you with Madge and Nora, courageous little ladies. You reassured her. I heard you myself."

"It seems so pitifully inadequate . . ."

"Perhaps so. But I remember what I said. As you no doubt recall, I said I wouldn't read the infernal thing for all the gold in England. Emmeline, on the other hand, would have traded all of England's wealth for what she found. Emmeline, always congenial, never the least aggressive, who always bowed to everyone else's bidding. She found strength to shame us all. I had to see why."

"Do you believe it?"

"I don't know. What I know is that Emmeline believed, and changed from a pleasant, passive non-entity to a veritable Joan of Arc. What I know is that I can no longer dismiss the book as a foregone triviality of blasphemous origin. I am ashamed that I could take poor Emmeline's faith so lightly."

"Where do we stand, then? What next, Henry?"

Again, Henry drew in a deep breath and held it in thought before exhaling. Clearly uneasy, he spoke slowly.

"Heber Kimball told us that he was a man, and man can deceive us. Don't look to me or any other creature of flesh, was essentially his advice. Flesh can deceive us. God, he said, is our only chance for knowledge, our only certainty."

"But 'E ain't 'ere!" Madge wailed.

"Quite right, Madge. And on the other hand, He is here." Seeing Madge's face, he could not suppress a smile. "Yes, He is, Madge. He has to be here. Emmeline found Him, and so did Heber. He has to be accessible."

"Wot?"

"I mean He can be here. He can speak to us as He spoke to Emmeline. Remember her letter? She said He spoke to her. I don't have her exact words, but it was something like hearing Him without hearing the timbre of His voice. Probably couldn't tell if He was tenor or baritone."

"Or soprano." Lydia couldn't resist.

"Point is, she heard Him, heard His reassurance, and it was enough to make her stronger than Rupert or her parents or the whole blasted society that tried to deny her the right to her faith."

"I don't know wot yer means wif 'Is not bein' 'ere and 'earin' of 'Is voice and the like, but wot I reads is good, in't it? Ain't nuffin' sinful wiv the readin' of the book, is there?"

"No, Madge, we're not sinning," Lydia affirmed. "What Henry is suggesting, I think, is now that we've read it . . ."

"But I ain't finished!"

"You've read enough to know whether you believe it or not," Lydia ventured.

"Believe it? Well, I never din't believe. Course I believes it. Din't no one just make it up, did they?"

"That's the question. Is it a true record or is it fabricated? You know, fiction," Lydia said.

"Wot's that?"

Henry chuckled but didn't try to explain fiction. "Now that we have read it, all or most of it, we have to find out if it's true."

"I think it's true!" Madge asserted.

"I'm afraid perhaps it is," Henry proffered a bit ruefully. "Not a very comfortable thought, is it? But I must know more. It's not enough, considering all the consequences, just to allow for the possibility."

"How do we . . ."

"Follow the indications, I suppose. Do what Heber suggested, and the other one. You remember, Lydia, toward the end."

"Oh, the one with the name that ends in *i*, like the Italian names. Moroni, wasn't it?" She laughed. "He wasn't Italian, was he?"

"Hardly, I should think. But he's the one with the plan, the, um, recipe, the same one Heber gave us." He appeared to be having difficulty talking about it. "I wish there were historical records, something to verify . . ."

"But there aren't," Lydia concluded. "Besides, records can be falsified, too. Verification is impossible."

"Yes, unless you can trust Heber and Moroni. I won't—can't trust the translator . . . What's his name? Smith. He's hardly a disinterested party, and besides, he's not within consulting distance."

Madge looked baffled. "I don't know wot yer mean," she admitted shamefacedly.

"He means we need to pray," Lydia simplified.

"That all? Wot's so 'ard about prayin'?" She remembered the vicar's prayers. "Oh," she said. She thought she understood the difficulty. The prayers she remembered were uttered in a register largely beyond both her preparation and inclination. "I don't know 'ow ter pray, neiver."

Madge's innocence relieved Henry a little. He was less uneasy and less harried when he could smile, and he suddenly found a way of postponing immediate action.

"Tell you what," he suggested. "Let's keep reading and pondering on our own, and perhaps praying alone, until Madge finishes the book."

"I reads fearful slow, I do," she said, blushing.

"We can keep reading each night, just like we have been," Lydia offered. "I can help you."

"Don't feel bad about slowing us down on this, Madge," Henry said. "Fact is, I want more time. I want to read it again. Some of it. All of it . . . How the devil did I get involved? I think I may be wishing I never had."

"Too late, Henry. Emmeline's real."

"How can a person who was always so innocuously undefined suddenly become the most potent motivator in our lives? Seems preposterous. What she gave us is . . ."

"Henry, I know you're frustrated. So am I. But Emmeline– You're not being fair to her."

"What?"

"You called her a 'pleasant non-entity' a minute ago and now she's 'innocuously undefined.' She was my dearest friend. That defines her quite endearingly to me. One doesn't have to be assertive and overpowering to etch a deep impression, and she always mattered far more than to be labeled as a 'pleasant non-entity.'"

"Ah. You're right, of course. Sorry. What I meant was, she seemed too mild to create all the upheaval for us. She's given us all a massive headache."

"Too massive to ignore. We need a remedy, not criticism of Emmeline, who's innocent of any ill intent."

"Yes. More time. I want more time, and we'll talk about it again when Madge finishes."

⁂

Henry went about his business as he always had, but a worried taciturnity had settled on him. On the occasions, too rare to suit him, when he had time with his children, he was playful and gentle as ever, but pensive. He was very careful to be patient and gentle with Lydia, and never scolded Madge or complained to Mrs. Folsum, but Lydia could discern changes in him, changes she thought she understood, for her own life had also changed.

The rain mumbled against the windows and chilled the air inside Henry's shop. He put on the heavy smock he wore when it grew cold but not quite cold enough to require lighting any more fire than was necessary for his forge. He left Hector in charge of the work that was underway and walked to one of the windows. That morning the clouds had rolled in and dulled the morning light. By noon rain started with a soft monologue that lasted for an hour and then increased to a kind of frenzy, rattling the windows with its fury. Now it was back to the monologue level but heavier than at noon. Steady, stubborn, smotheringly monotonous, it prattled on like a stodgy sermon that had no trajectory and no hint of closure. His shop occupied a generous section of his barn, with a large sign, generations old, that read GLENDRAKE, WHEELWRIGHTS AND BODY BUILDERS. From the door of the shop, a flagstone path led to the back door of his house. The window appeared to be in perpetual melt, distorting the view, but through the blur the flagstones glistened as rain washed across their surface and continued the peppering that made them appear to dance. The crystalline ripples absorbed him, hypnotized him almost. He could see the garden in indistinct blotches, flourishing in late summer, probably relishing the lavish moisture. How could one tell if the grass, flowers, shrubs, and trees ever thanked the earth for her nurturing anchor or the skies for their gratuitous quenching?

Soon, his thoughts dropped a curtain between what his eyes saw and where his mind focused. The path, trees, flowers, grass, and shrubs were still there, but lost in the surge of other concerns.

What did he owe to Emmeline's memory? No, that was not the question. Don't blame Emmeline. The question was, what could he do with the legacy she had left them? Was that still blaming Emmeline? No, Emmeline left them her faith, her own gentle, stubborn courage, and the book. Hang the book. No, he didn't mean that. The book wasn't responsible either, but it was an infernal nuisance. How uncomplicated living had been before the book showed up next to Lydia's plate.

It would be so easy, so comfortable just to forget Emmeline's fortuitous encounter with the Mormons—the missionaries, Heber and Amos, and the book, the omnipresent book.

But there was no dismissing any of them. Emmeline's conversion was real and her death confirmed it; Heber and Amos were not ghosts but men with a mission. And the book, the constant, nagging reminder, the palpable, wheedling, cloying presence of the book that he could no longer ignore and whose message he could not in conscience fully deny. Did he believe? He wished he did not. Did he? If only he did not. Did he?

He would have to know. He would have to explore until he knew.

And if he discovered what he hoped he would not? What if the thing he had feared without facing the fear should become a reality? What if he reached the moment when he would have to say, as Emmeline had, "I can no longer question, I must concede, I cannot deny?" The consequences swept through his brain like a ravaging army. His business could–no doubt would–suffer beyond retrieve, his friends would avoid him, his sisters would launch a maelstrom of protest, and Lydia's family . . .

Squire Smirthwaite, with all his broad-mindedness and tolerance for his daughter's proclivities, could never countenance such an egregious affront to his position. And worst of all, perhaps, Henry's children would suffer humiliation and rejection. In all of

England, he would not find a corner where he might be welcome without reservation.

Henry took his lugubrious thoughts to bed with him that night, and after a brief devotional, he and Lydia put out the candle and lay quietly together for a few minutes. Henry broke the silence.

"Lydia, tell me specifically what draws you to this book." She knew that "this book" referred to the Book of Mormon. He continued, "Why are we even considering the possibility that it may be valid?"

"Well, you have to concede, it has certainly changed our perspective, hasn't it? Emmeline. Madge. Me. And you, Henry. Even you."

"If that is so, *why* is it so? What has changed us?"

"One writer in the book calls it a *mighty* change. Remember?"

"But what can you point to in particular? Any one thing?"

"Perhaps not any *one* thing. Well, yes I can. For example, Madge and I spoke of a very short passage that flies in the face of all the solemn, pious sooth-sayers that I have never been able to abide, any better than you have. The ones who fear that God despises cheeriness. It says, 'Man is that he might have joy.' " Henry nodded but kept his peace. Lydia plunged onward: "I like it. I'm particularly pleased when I hear, or read, a prophet who justifies what I have always believed, sometimes in spite of what the vicar may say."

"Such as what, lass?" Henry pursued.

"Oh, you know. The vicar sometimes speaks as if . . ."

"I didn't mean 'such as what does the vicar say.' I meant such as what do you find in the Book of Mormon that you find so compelling?"

"Such as . . . Oh, why are you so insistent? Surely you don't expect me to remember where to find it."

"Then just tell me what you remember. It may be that I've already read it and thought it over myself."

"Well, early on, I remember reading that all men—I noticed that it said all *men* and remarked to myself that it's a man's world wherever you are . . ." She felt Henry squirm beside her. "All right,

I know, it means all humankind. Anyway, it says all have equal privilege. Before God, all are equal. Just a few paragraphs further on, the writer makes his point again, this time more specifically. God, he says, remembers all of His children, male *and* female, black, white, slave, heathen, Jew, or whatever."

"That's hardly new doctrine, though, is it?"

"No, probably not, but it's certainly clear. Clearer than what I remember from our Bible reading. And it really *would* be a mighty change if we practiced it"

"Oh, come now, lass. The Bible makes it plain that if one seeks, he—or *she* . . ." he punched the syllable with brutal emphasis. . . "shall find. That means anyone, I expect. Christ indicated that *God* is there; *we* must approach *Him*. 'How oft would I have gathered you . . . but *ye* would not.'"

"I know. We both believe that. Kings are no higher than peasants in God's heaven. But we don't live that way."

"Quite true, my little aristocrat. We've made a muddle of things here below, haven't we?"

"Isn't there a king—yes there is. The one who had a tower built so he could preach to his people before he died. He said he tilled the earth with his own hands so he wouldn't be a burden to his subjects." She giggled. "Imagine the Queen in gardening clothes!" she laughed and then grew suddenly sober and socked Henry on the shoulder. "What do you mean, you peasant clod? 'My little aristocrat,' indeed!"

Henry chuckled. "Thought for a moment you had missed my point."

"I told Madge about my friend Roseanne, whom you never had the fortune to meet." She sighed. "The most delightful friend I ever had. Aside from my husband, of course. And she was a traveling player, with no connections whatsoever."

Henry nodded in the darkness. "No connections whatsoever. Yet she connected so thoroughly with you that you remember her almost as vividly as you remember Emmeline." His contemplative smile was not visible in the darkness, but Lydia could feel it as he laid his arm across her in the bed and drew closer to her.

"Thank you, my dear little aristocrat, for believing that God has made us equal."

Reading sessions went on for several weeks, and one evening Madge announced with a blush and a twinkle that she had finished the whole book. Henry smiled at her.

"And what do you think of it, lass?" he asked her.

She answered slowly. "Like I said afore. Ain't changed wot I said."

Henry nodded, almost grimly. It would be easier for Madge. Belief would cost her less. She certainly would never be denied a place in their household, so her employment was secure, and her position in society could diminish, but to what? Only the beggars had less than those who occupied the lowest ranks of service. In a way, she was more fortunate than he and Lydia. Her belief would not ostracize her. Well, perhaps it would, but the effect would be less devastating, he reasoned. Her world was smaller.

Lydia interrupted his musings: "Henry, we have all read the book now. What's next?"

Henry drew in a long breath. It was the exact reaction Lydia had expected. Now, she thought, he will make his pronouncement. But he made no pronouncement.

"There's no arguing with it, is there?" he asked.

"With what?"

"You know. The recipe. The instrucion Heber and the Italian prophet prescribed."

"The Italian . . .?"

"Moroni." He pronounced it, as they had from the beginning, as if the *i* were a long *e*, as an Italian would. "They both say we have to ask beyond our earthly sources, since all of those may be suspect."

"We've been reading together. Alone too, of course. But— shouldn't we pray together about it? Of course, I don't mind if you think it's best to do it quietly and personally, but we've been so much together..."

Henry thought of Madge and wondered if she had ever prayed independently. It wouldn't do them any injury to do as Lydia suggested. He was sure she was thinking of Madge.

"I suppose we can do it together. Of course we can," he said.

"Like the day we knelt with Mr. Kimball and Mr. Fielding and..." Lydia began.

"Yes, but Heber isn't here now, is he? Who will be the one to..."

"You, of course. Who else?"

Henry frowned, saying nothing, and then slowly, self-consciously, he moved from his chair and knelt on the floor. Lydia and Madge followed.

Henry fumbled and scratched through his thoughts, searching for a beginning. He started awkwardly, addressing God directly.

"God..." he stopped, not knowing what to say next. He thought of the vicar, remembering his prayers as a kind of recitation. Henry had nothing to recite. Then he remembered Heber and his frank and informal reverence. "Father in heaven, we need help from You." Heber had prayed using an archaic "thee" and "thou" address, but it reminded Henry more of Shakespeare than God, and he felt more comfortable with modern vernacular. But the memory of Heber's easy, almost familiar fluency settled his thoughts, and he launched his prayer:

"The help we need is knowledge. Our experience with Emmeline has sobered us a great deal. Emmeline believed, and we have taken her courage to heart and read the Book of Mormon. We are not willing to take anyone's word that it's a true book; not even Emmeline's. We have been advised by a missionary to take only Your word, and that's why we're praying to You this way. Can You help us, please? We have all read the book, and Moroni tells us to do what Heber Kimball said to do. Is this book true, and did You send it to us?" He paused, then ended almost in a whisper. "In the name of Christ Jesus, amen."

He did not open his eyes at once. He heard a quiet sniffle from Madge's direction and nothing from Lydia's. He opened his eyes and confirmed that Madge was weeping. Lydia, her hands together on the arm of the easy chair where she was kneeling, rested her head on her hands with her eyes closed, motionless, moved too deeply to move.

Henry knew that their lives would never be the same.

Another rainy afternoon, and Henry's restiveness, he could tell, had begun to wear on Hector and the young apprentice, Malcolm. He distanced himself from them for a few moments and then walked back to where they were working in time to interrupt a lecture Hector was delivering to his junior associate. Henry's preemptory voice rescued the boy.

"Hector, I'm going for a ride. The rain's slowed a bit."

"Still very wet for ridin', sir," Hector observed.

"Can't be helped. I'll wear my raincoat, the waterproof wrap. Well, as waterproof as they can make it. Could you get my horse ready?"

"I'll see to it, sir," Hector said, turning to the apprentice. "Malcolm?"

"Yes, sir?"

"Fetch the master's 'orse, would you?"

Henry returned to the window to gaze again across the rain-washed landscape. His apprentice and journeyman, both silently puzzling over the master's introspective demeanor and his sudden need to venture into the wet and chill of the afternoon, prepared his horse while he remained at the window. He rarely left the preparation of his mount exclusively to his help, but today he seemed quite indifferent, distracted. They wisely asked no questions.

Henry put on his heavy winter wrap and then slung the oil-treated raincoat over it, mounted his mare and turned her toward the gate. The rain still continued but had indeed "slowed a bit." He let the mare choose her gait as he reined her toward the vicarage.

Hugh saw him approach and hurried to meet him with an umbrella before he dismounted.

"Not a congenial afternoon for riding, Henry. What urgency brings you to my doorstep?"

"Sorry to surprise you, but what I need can't seem to wait. What am I interrupting that probably shouldn't have to be postponed?"

"Nothing that can't be postponed. I was reading and fussing a bit with my paperwork. Nothing more. Hurry in! I'm afraid this umbrella is losing my respect. I'm wet from the knees down."

They turned the horse over to the vicar's stable boy and went inside where Temperance met them with hot coffee.

"I'm here to have audience with my pastor," Henry said.

Temperance smiled. "Even my brother! Do you know how many times a week I'm excluded from all the juicy gossip I could spread if only I knew what was going on?"

Hugh chuckled. "So you know why it has to be private, don't you?"

"I'm not a gossip!"

"I know, my dear, but you're not the vicar, either. Unfortunately for your curiosity, I am. But I'm not so sure there's anything fortunate in that circumstance, either."

"Sorry to lay another burden on you, Hugh, but I would appreciate your hearing a problem you surely can't solve."

"That would be a first, wouldn't it? Let's go to the library. Thanks for the coffee, Temperance, my love."

In the library, Hugh lost no time with idle patter, but his question was as original as green for the color of grass.

"What's your problem, Henry?"

Henry drew in his breath, held it, as usual when he was perplexed, and then exhaled, finally ready to speak.

"It is a spiritual problem. Larger by far than I ever could have imagined. You know the book I told you about? The one Emmeline Plowhurst got from the Mormons?"

"I know only what you told me. I know that Lydia was somewhat taken with it, wasn't she?"

"Not just Lydia, Hugh. We've all read it now. Lydia and I, and Madge."

"Madge?"

"Yes. Lydia taught her to read, you know."

"How extraordinary!"

"She's a smart little lass. Never had a day of schooling; never a single advantage did life offer her. When Lydia found her, she was alone in the street, destined, I suppose, to learn how to pick pockets or wind up in an orphanage or . . . well, that's not important. We all spent time reading, and this is the problem, Hugh: We all knelt together to ask God for guidance, because we certainly didn't want to believe that there could be any authenticity to the book's claims. To a person, we stood after our prayer to God–the only one I could ever trust for an answer–and knew, without ever another word, that the book is of God. No man could have written it alone and produced what we felt and knew." He paused, reading disbelief, dismay, perhaps horror, in Hugh's face. "I told you, you wouldn't find a solution to this one."

Hugh did not answer. He dropped his head into his hands and sat that way, silent in what appeared to Henry utter wretchedness. Finally he lifted his head.

"It's the premise, Henry. Just as I told Lydia. Surely you remember? No argument can stand on a false premise."

"Who determines that the premise is false, Hugh? You? Your ecclesiastical superior? King Henry VIII? (Heaven help us!) Who?"

"The Lord Himself. The Bible He left us. St. John, in the final verses of the Apocalypse."

"Which was written before the books of the Bible were assembled, which simply means that St. John made reference to the writing *he* had just completed, the book we call the Apocalypse, not the entire Bible."

"Do you pretend to teach *me* what's in the Bible, Henry?"

"Mercy, no, Hugh." His expression was pure irony. Then he drew his brows together tightly.

"I didn't think that was the point. I thought we were trying to answer a question which you seem willing to dodge by taking refuge in your superior position as an ordained minister. If you insist on doing that, we never will deal with my question, will we?"

Hugh stared hard at him, his face muscles tense. Henry sighed.

"Never mind, Hugh. If all we're about here is the game of 'Who knows more than who?' we're wasting each other's time, aren't we? Sorry to intrude on your tranquil pursuits. My best to Temperance." He rose and strode toward the door.

"Wait, Henry. Don't . . . don't be stalking off like that. I don't mean to seem authoritative . . ."

"Then what the devil do you mean? I asked who made the premise a false one and you assume that I know without the need to ask, or you want me to accept it as a given without question. That's just what I did at first. Then Lydia persuaded me with the simple logic that she had read something I had not and was therefore better prepared to judge it than I. The very logic I would have used had the roles been reversed. Now, if you mean to imply that God was the one who decided the premise was false, when did He decide it? To whom did He confide it?"

"It's . . . traditionally accepted that the Bible is God's word, and contains the fullness of His law."

"I no longer trust tradition," Henry said. "Tradition was what motivated Plowhurst. His wife is dead, and worth more dead than his miserable, tradition-loving hide. It was the Jews' perverted worship of tradition that justified the crucifixion of the Savior. Don't speak to me of tradition."

An asphyxiating silence filled the library. Henry spoke again softly. "Good-bye, Hugh." He opened the door.

"Henry, please don't leave. I allowed this to get out of hand without ever hearing you, didn't I? You know it's blasted hard having to parade about as though you had all the answers, and sometimes I suppose it's just easier to hide behind the facade. You struck the exact chord, I'm afraid; I *am* hiding behind that comfortable image of authority, aren't I? Blast it, let me cast aside the cloth for a moment. It might frighten you, and I wonder—and maybe I fear—that I might find it more comfortable. If you'll listen to me, I'll listen to you."

Henry paused, his hand on the doorknob. He laughed, a low, ironic rumble. "I don't know what you'd want to say to me, but if you have no more faith in my ability to solve your problems than I have in yours to solve mine, we'll just have a fine empty chat." He stepped back inside the room and shut the door.

"I'll settle for that. Just don't walk out in angry frustration. I guess I want you to hear of a few of my own. I–ah–I haven't had a restful night since I learned of poor Mrs. Plowhurst's death. You remember, I promised I would speak with her husband, and I went straightway to his house to fulfill my promise. He received me with reluctant cordiality and assured me that he knew exactly what he was doing and would soon obtain the results he expected; felt that victory was just another day away. He was so sure he was justified that . . . Henry, I feel deep shame that I was not more forceful. Perhaps my visit only served to intensify Plowhurst's resolve. I have tried to convince myself since poor Emmeline died that I did all I could. I fear I'm lying to myself. She did not have to die, and I should have prevented it. Those are the thoughts that murder my sleep."

"I suppose we do expect too much of those whose work is our shepherding. I very much doubt that you could have altered the results of Rupert's narrow perception."

"Thank you for trying, Henry. The fact remains, I did not pursue the matter vigorously. I did not imagine it was that serious."

"You and all the rest of us." Henry laughed, a short, bitter sound rather like a snort. "Do you know, Dr. Driscoll, my crusty old friend and our able physician who claims to be an atheist, expressed more sympathetic understanding for Emmeline than her own father. What are we, Hugh? Doesn't our religion allow for any differences, any other view than the one we hold?"

"It's just that a woman should listen . . ."

"Exactly! Women are supposed to be dependent upon us, submissive, inferior by nature or divine decree. And I live with a woman who is more than my equal. I don't mean her superior social rank, I mean her mind, her judgment, her courage, her vision. None of us would allow that Emmeline was anything but deluded. Even Lydia at first, but she valued Emmeline as a friend, enough to at least explore her motives. I dismissed her out of hand."

Hugh stood and walked to the window, listening, absorbed.

"Lydia made a discovery, and I resisted so strenuously I almost . . . well, I know better, now," Henry continued. "Hugh, Emmeline could not yield because she found God. Can either of us be as certain, certain enough to die for our belief?"

Hugh stared silently out the window. When he spoke, he did not turn to face Henry.

"I have spent my life searching for God. Since I was old enough to command a measure of trust in my power to reason, I have searched. I was fortunate. My father was wealthy, though my family boasts no title, no more than yours, but I was given the privilege of following my inclinations by attending divinity school." He turned now, and Henry regarded him intently.

"I concede, I could not find God in my studies," Hugh continued. "I discovered that, for me, the only way to reach God was through service to His children. I overcame the terrible impediment of my shyness by imitating the style of one of my mentors, and could only manage to conquer my fears by pretending that the sermons I prepared were delivered in his voice." Again he turned his face toward the window. "I have little faith in my command of the Bible; I cannot reconcile the inconsistencies among the scriptures, tradition, reason, and authority. If poor Mrs. Plowhurst heard the voice of God in another way, and was sure it was His voice, I can only envy her. Even in death she is fortunate if she died assured." He paused, again turning to face Henry. "Are you telling me, Henry, that you have found God?"

"I believe I have. I'm trembling even as I say it, because I know the consequences. I believe Emmeline discovered that God has spoken again."

Hugh turned toward the window again, seemingly fastened to a point in space.

"Can I interest you in the book, Hugh?" Henry asked softly.

Hugh did not answer, and silence grew heavy. Finally he said with quiet finality, "No. I could not abandon what I have discovered. I must be engaged in serving God's children as I am able and try to finish what I have begun. St. James calls it the 'royal law.' What if I believed what you seem to believe, Henry? Could I convert my entire parish? I would do more harm than you can imagine. I would disrupt the entire community and probably drive away no small number of those who depend upon me. I have a calling here. It may be as inferior and false as my preaching style, but it's better than abandoning this flock to satisfy my own hunger, if indeed it can be satisfied." He smiled. It was a mirthless, sad smile. "Do you remember the traveling players who came through Eccleston last summer?"

"No. I heard Temperance speak of them. I didn't see them."

"They had a series of shows—acts, I suppose—of several varieties. Rather old-fashioned, but they made us laugh, sometimes weep—changed our routine and entertained us for a few minutes. One of the actors had a short sketch for children. Gave a very good performance. Animated, slap-stick, funny. Captivated the little ones. I learned that this actor's wife was ill—I found out because they summoned me to attend her spiritually before she succumbed. Tuberculosis, I expect. She looked terribly wasted. That actor did his job. Made the children happy. Never shed a tear while on stage and then broke down completely after the show. Loved his wife. Loved her. But he did his job."

It was Henry now who kept silent.

"I can't doff my costume, can I Henry?" Hugh said.

~~~

No discussion had been necessary following the epiphanic evening prayer, but Lydia noted the lack of assurance in Henry's eyes, the greater-than-ever pensiveness that weighed upon him. She knew that having reached a conviction he would have to decide upon his course of action, but she could not fully understand his moods. She held her peace when she saw him leave his shop on several occasions without explanation, sensing that her normal loquacity and need for communication must wait for a season. Time would ripen the moment for Henry to reveal his concerns.

Nightly readings in the privacy of their bedroom went on as usual for Lydia and Henry, but the substance of the ritual varied now. The Bible shared time with the Book of Mormon. In fact, the Book of Mormon, being new and less familiar, claimed the greater share of their attention, as they felt the urgency to grasp the concepts it articulated, most often echoing those of the Bible but with a fresh view and occasionally presenting new concepts, always angled toward the understanding of Christ's universal mission as Lord and Redeemer.

Madge worked every day without mentioning the prayer and the vigil that ended with Henry's "amen," but a bond even stronger than before developed between her and Lydia. She continued her reading as often as she could, and her skill improved steadily. She awaited impatiently her trips to the market because they gave her access to Nora.

Early one Sunday, Henry announced that they would not attend church at the vicar's parish but in the warehouse on Parr Lane, close to the Sherbourn tannery in Eccleston.

Sixteen

Madge's time off from work had no programmed schedule. She knew she could expect consideration anytime she felt a need for vacation or rest, but without family of her own and few acquaintances, her needs outside Horse Stone House were spare indeed. Her world expanded considerably when the family began attending worship services with the Mormons, where she found new friends, but Nora continued to be her closest and dearest associate outside Horse Stone. Madge considered herself a member of the family but recognized and accepted her obligations of servitude, never imagining she was beyond Lydia's or Henry's control, and she never chafed at their expectations. She knew her place in the rigidly leveled society to which she was born and felt privileged that she had a secure niche within it.

Nora's situation was different. She could expect regular days of reprieve from her services and was not free to request leisure of any stripe outside the two days a month she was allotted. She had but one sibling, a brother, married, expecting a child, living precariously as a dock worker in Liverpool, and too short of leisure or inclination to spend time with her. Most often, she visited Madge on her days off, frequently spending the day at Horse Stone, but occasionally she and Madge would shop in Eccleston—which consisted mostly of browsing without purchasing—or take walks through the countryside.

A little over a year after Emmeline's death, Nora dropped in on the Glendrakes and asked permission to visit Madge. It was a familiar pattern. If Lydia was beset by tasks she could not postpone, Nora would join her and Madge, and among them they would dispatch the chore and Lydia would then excuse Madge for the rest of the day. Usually, she would simply dismiss her to do whatever she wished with Nora, as she did on the day in question. They prepared a basket lunch, and the girls set out for the countryside to enjoy an afternoon of sunshine and chatter. Lydia watched them leave, smiling her own pleasure and wondering a little how she could feel so deeply for little Madge whose condition was so clearly inferior. Such inequities troubled her, especially as she contemplated her own husband's qualities, superior by any measure to all the men she knew within her own class. Only by accident of birth was he inferior, and she could fathom that only as an artificial assignation, quite arbitrary and unnatural.

Conversation between Madge and Nora always wandered over varied topics but never failed at some point to touch Emmeline. Nora was aware of Madge's new religious leaning, which originated with Emmeline, whom Nora had served and loved. She knew of the evening readings at Horse Stone and the prayer they shared that clinched their resolve and led them to affiliate with the Mormons, though they had not accepted baptism. She knew of Madge's feelings for the Book of Mormon, Emmeline's own touchstone of faith, and envied Madge's ability to read it, a privilege she could not claim.

Summer dazzled the meadow, but with a bit of amphibiology. An occasional breeze tickled the wild daffodils, long since bloomless but still standing, their spear-leaves already showing yellow at their base on the bare stem. The blossoms had been yellow too, but brilliant with life and shaped like the bell of a trumpet, a blaring assertion, yet too small and daintily ruffled for insolence. In spring, the daffodils' yellow blazoned assurance; in summer it whimpered vulnerability. Summer was the season for the robust splendor of hollyhocks and roses and a few late blooms still clinging to the wisteria vine, but spring flowers were dying.

Nora sighed contentedly as she sat with an abandon which slightly compromised the dignity she would have guarded had she not been sure they were alone. She lay back on the slope of the hill they had chosen for their lunch site, spread-eagle, her skirts unfurled about her.

"I ain't 'ad a walk like this in more'n a year. Me bloomin' legs feels wobbly, like me bones 'as turned ter butter."

"Go on! Yer 'as ter be on yer feet all day, same as me. Wot's the differnce twixt walkin' a bit and fetchin' in an' abaht the 'ouse? We ain't ones fer sittin' idle-like, you and me."

"Takes a lady fer sittin'. A nob. Not the likes o' us."

"Mrs. Glendrake in't no nob. Not like that. Not 'er. She does work, same as me."

"'Er mother don't, least wise not no work as takes more'n orderin' an' complainin'. Mrs. Plow'hurst, now, she were different. More like your mistress, she was."

"Misses 'er, doncher?"

"She were gentle. Never no lookin' at yer wiv them eyes as would kill flies in mid-flight, as 'er 'usband did. Sometimes Mrs. Smirthwaite, too. Like yer was a beetle what 'ad crawled out o' the woodwork and dared ter share space wiv yer."

Madge laughed. "Mrs. Glendrake is quality, same as 'er mother, but she don't mind gettin' 'er 'ands dirty, and she don't make me feel as I ain't worth nuffin'. Taught me to read, she did."

"Ar, that'd be sumfink. The devil'd 'av ter take communion afore you'd catch Mrs. Smirthwaite teachin' one of us ter whistle."

"I remember once, though, I seen Mrs. Glendrake puttin' on them high airs wiv a gent what tried ter 'elp us ter a seat in the meetin' place where Mrs. Plow'urst used ter go ter church."

"The ware'ouse in Eccleston? It's where you go instead of the vicar's church, now, ain't it?"

"She 'ad that look, the kind as would kill flies, and the man fair wilted. I see 'im there of Sundays, when we go back, but 'e keeps 'is distance from me mistress, 'e does. I seen 'er smile at 'im, kind o' friendly like, maybe wantin' ter make amends, but 'e don't dare come too close. A good man, 'e is, too, says I."

Nora lay silently on the hill, and Madge began talking of something else, but Nora clearly was not ready to abandon the topic of Madge's new church.

"Wot's the difference in yer new church fum the vicar's church?" Her question interrupted Madge in mid-sentence. "Wot was Mr. Plow'urst so puckered abaht? Fair foamin' at the mouth 'e was, and sayin' awful things abaht them as went to where yer goin', but nobody never said as why."

"Don't know nuffin' abaht wot Mr. Plow'urst 'ad in 'is craw. Don't know wot all the fuss is. There's differnces, right enough. Cozier-like. And they 'ave the book, the one Mrs. Plow'urst gave me mistress. The Book of Mormon, you remembers."

"I remembers the name of it right enough, but I don't know nuffink else. Can't know wot's in it coz I can't read."

Madge's sense of superiority held no nuance of one-upmanship, just a wave of gratitude to Lydia and Henry for emancipating her mind with an ability denied to Nora and most of her class. Her response was unpretentious and sincere.

"If we 'ad more time, I could read it to yer. I reads it, some of it, every day. But wiv you livin' at the Smirthwaites and me livin' at 'Orse Stone 'Ouse, wou'nt be no use. Exceptin' fer these days wen we walks a bit, we only sees each other on market days fer a minute, maybe two, and there ain't time fer sittin' to read . Um . . . Do yer go ter church Sundays?"

"Most o' the time. Mrs. Smirthwaite allows as it's good fer us 'service girls' ter git our religious teachin' and expects us ter go ter 'ear the vicar."

Madge felt another serge of warmth for the privileges luck or providence had bequeathed her. Church was a family affair, now more than ever. She had obligations even at church, but she shared them with Lydia and felt as much a part of the family circle as the children she tended. Nora's place in the grand Smirthwaite mansion gave her greater stature among others of their station, but Nora worked behind barriers of rigid class separation, relegated to a position just slightly above the master's livestock, and even that might be open to debate, because the expectations of superior intelligence and understanding entailed upon one's having been born human occasioned more abuse than the master ever exercised on his horses or cows. Madge recognized her own meager status but never felt belittled by it. It was what life dealt, without explanation or apology. Nora was reminded constantly of her inferiority, not through unkindness but through indifference, apparent in attitude, posture, or inference. Never included in family concerns, never consulted, never considered worthy of an opinion, always a distant object, a possession, largely insensible.

Madge appeared to be struggling. At length she emerged from the conflict victorious.

"Wot if yer came wiv us ter Emmeline's church?" she asked Nora. "Mr. Glendrake wou'nt mind drivin' 'is carriage by yer place, ain't far out o' 'is way, and yer already expected ter go ter church, so yer wou'nt 'ave ter ask no permission."

Nora thought it over briefly, beamed, and nodded. As they walked home, they discussed the anticipated pleasure of another regular occasion to come together.

Later, Madge put the question to Lydia, who acquiesced immediately. She felt obligated to Nora and approved heartily of Madge's association with her. They had enlisted Nora in Emmeline's cause, which had occasioned the loss of her position, but Lydia suffered no remorse over that. She knew Nora was grateful for the change. Still, they had inconvenienced her considerably, and Lydia welcomed the chance to favor her.

Henry demurred. He did not object to Nora's going with them in principle, yet he could not dismiss his reservations.

"You know, it's only a matter of time before your parents discover where we're taking her, and they'll also discover our involvement. What are you going to say to them?"

"What I have always said: that I am free to make my own choices."

"This time, it won't be that simple. Oh, I know, it wasn't simple when we got married either, but this will be far worse."

Lydia bit her lip. "Why should it be?"

"Because . . . Well, you know why. It's one thing to marry outside your station and quite another to abandon your belief in God."

"But we aren't! In fact . . ."

"I know, we're being as true to Him as we can, but you'll never convince your family of that. Any more than Emmeline could convince Rupert."

She did not answer, and Henry stood silent. At length, Lydia murmured, "We haven't consented to be baptized."

"I know," he answered simply.

"We were baptized Christians before we ever knew of the Mormons. Why do we have to . . . ?"

"Lydia, my love, do we believe what they're preaching or don't we?"

The question unnerved her, and she answered sharply. "Aren't we attending meetings with them? We associate with them, we go every Sunday. You know I wouldn't do that if I didn't believe."

Henry appeared to ignore the sharpness in her voice and went on in the same level tone: "But you don't choose to believe it when they tell you that your baptism as an infant in the Church of England had no validity in the true church of God, the restored church with authentic authority?"

"But . . ."

"*Authentic*, Lydia. They're telling us that priesthood authority was lost with the disappearance of the organization. The line was broken."

Frustration had her close to tears. "Well, couldn't they— couldn't they be wrong about that? Do they have to be right every time they cross a *t* or dot an *i*?"

"I don't know where to draw a line, I'm afraid. If they're wrong about baptism, are they also wrong about all the other revelations we say we believe in? Face it, lass, we do or we don't. It's easier to insist to everyone that we are curious but not committed, and that's why we go to church with them, but it's not honest, is it?"

"Emmeline was never baptized."

"But she would have been, wouldn't she?"

Lydia looked blackly at him and nodded. Henry continued: "We have to think what we're going to do, love. It's not a simple choice. You know that I'll no doubt lose my business."

"What? Why would you lose your business?"

"Just imagine—would Rupert Plowhurst come to me for service or new wheels?" He paused, his eyebrows raised, mildly inquisitive. "I know, he's an extreme case, but people don't trust their business to traitors or heretics, and that's how we'll appear." He smiled at her. "Just remember how Superintendent Pembroke explained why the police couldn't intervene with Emmeline when she was merely badgered and bullied but not yet butchered. We don't have to be heretics or blasphemers to be accused of it, and that's enough to put us on the road to the workhouse."

"Then . . . but what can we do?" she asked, fearing to hear his answer and suddenly understanding why her husband's moods had become pensive, his words fewer and his attitude distant. Born to privilege and wealth, she had never really considered that life could hang precariously on public endorsement. She remembered how in a fit of pique she had once threatened to leave, avowing that she would accept service if she had to, and now she knew that her threat had been shallow and unthinking. Life with Henry had meant adjusting to a more meager endowment, less pampering, fewer luxuries, but he had lavished affection, confidence, and praise on her, trusted her, given her freedom, made her a thoroughgoing partner in all that conjugality implies. With a jolt, she felt his loneliness, the demands upon a man who dared to challenge his society and marry above his station. She had peered fleetingly into the guarded precinct where anxieties prowled and scowled through the shadows, like caged wolves that saw freedom beyond their enclosure with yearning eyes and grudging resignation. She knew Henry could say with perfect sincerity that he would not choose any other course, but perhaps only because he had not seen an acceptable alternative. She could not let him know what she had just discovered. She shook her head, heaved a heavy sigh, and went on, dissimulating: "Well, what do we tell Nora? That she's better off not associating with us on Sundays?"

Henry grinned. "If she wants to stay comfortable, then that would be the best advice. But what if she wants to know, just as you did? What then?"

"Then she's welcome to our company any time, Sundays and all. Now what are we going to do about the Mormons? Are you going to allow Amos Fielding to baptize us?"

"Yes. In good time, if you're still convinced that it's true."

"I . . . I never thought much of all the consequences . . ." The confession was too revealing, but Henry did not notice.

"Neither of us has thought of all of them, love," he said gently.

"I still haven't changed my mind about the Book of Mormon."

"Can we feel as we do–I mean can we feel that it's true–without embracing it? Are you prepared to live hypocritically for the rest of your life?"

Lydia arched her brow in the best aristocratic fashion. She knew the art of dissimulation. "You put it so elegantly, Henry. Just tell me what our options are!"

"Seems to me integrity demands that we affiliate, don't you think?"

"You still haven't told me how we're going to manage."

"Because I don't know. But I have thought . . . Squire Farnsworth admires our farm. I think he'd buy it."

"Sell? Henry, for odd and bossy, that's absurd. How long would the money last? And when it's gone, what then?"

"The sale will give us passage to America, lass."

"Passage to . . . No, Henry. Leave England? *Leave England?* No, no, no, there has to be . . ."

"A better way? I've harrowed my brains raw trying to find it, and I can't. Our society is what it is, and I know what it will do to us. I keep telling myself that I don't lack courage–it will take plenty of that to uproot ourselves and settle in one of England's colonies, the rebellious one at that. But I know what our chances are here. I'm not wealthy. I have to earn my keep with my trade, and I have but one. If that trade drops off, what happens to my children? Or to you?"

"We'll be just as courageous as you are, Henry, and we will face whatever . . ."

"As outcasts? Beggars? Remember Emmeline. She *was* cast out, wasn't she? And shall we be treated differently? How shall we earn our bread as pariahs?"

She had no reply beyond wide-eyed disbelief.

"Are you wondering how it can be any better in America?" Henry went on. "I confess, I wonder the same thing. Amos says . . ."

"Amos is an Englishman! He's staying on, and if he can, surely we . . ."

"Amos is emigrating, Lydia. Leaving. He spoke at length with Heber and gathered all the intelligence he could about conditions. We'll be able to find land there, and we'll live with the Mormons in a community that believes as we do. We will have a community, Lydia, others who accept us. Outsiders probably won't like us any better there than here, but the members have gathered, and the prophet visits them, lives with them . . ."

"Oh, please don't take us away from home. At least don't force me to decide now. Please, let's see if we can't discover something better. I don't want to leave England. It would be . . ."

"It would be harsh and bitter. A challenge beyond any we have known, I suspect, but you have never dodged challenge, have you? You are equal it. To anything. No one stronger."

Lydia dropped her eyes and said nothing. She did not feel strong at all and even wished Henry could see how desolate she was. Perhaps his confidence was more terrifying than reassuring. Henry waited and then added, "But I'm not forcing it on you. It's just a possibility, I suppose. We'll let the notion settle on us for a while, what? See how it all looks later."

Seventeen

Henry drew close to Squire Farnsworth's handsome estate, a place he had been made to feel comfortable in. But at the moment he was not comfortable. He walked through the well-ordered gardens leading to the intimidating oak doors, massive, aristocratic, territorial. He had requested an audience, which the squire readily granted in an answering note delivered by his footman. The squire's obvious partiality toward Henry did not assuage Henry's raging uneasiness. In fact, he could not suppress the feelings of betrayal that rose to accuse him despite his conviction that he had no alternative.

The squire's butler admitted him with formal cordiality and bade him await the master in the withdrawing room. The squire appeared shortly, followed by the same butler with a tray of glasses and a decanter of port.

The old squire's gait now betrayed the ravages of rheumatism, and his bent posture was nothing like the resolute erectness of yesteryear. His eyes, however, blazing beneath bristling brows, showed no sign of diminished alertness. He greeted Henry warmly and offered him a glass of port, at which the butler filled the glasses without noting whether Henry accepted the offer or not and tendered the tray to the squire and his guest. Henry thanked him and sipped the rich sweetness that began immediately to warm away some of his uneasiness.

"Well, Henry lad, to what do I owe the pleasure of your visit?" The squire asked. Prolixity was not among the old man's characteristics.

"My circumstances have become very complex." Henry knew he too must come to the point. "I'm obliged to leave England, sir. I have my little farm, and I should like to sell it if I can, to meet expenses of transfer to America."

"Leave England? What do you mean, leave England?"

"It's a bit complicated, but in very short, I must pursue what I have come to know as God's will. To follow Him, as I know I must, I shall have to abandon these pleasant, familiar, and very nurturing home fires and try to kindle them abroad."

"I'm afraid I don't grasp a single tad nor tatter of what you're saying. Why can't you worship God right here at home? Do you suppose He changes shape in America? Or that He's more accessible there?"

"Not at all. It was here I discovered . . . well, I believe, sir, in fact I am quite certain, that my affiliation with the new sect I must embrace will drive a wedge between me and this English society that I love. My business will not survive."

"Then why . . . ?"

"It's not going to be easy to understand, I'm afraid. Let me try, as briefly as I can . . ."

"Take whatever time you need, Henry. I'm not pressed."

"But I can't feel at ease wasting your time, can I, sir? I'll get to the point. I have read a book, a translation from ancient documents discovered in America."

"The documents were discovered in America?"

"Yes, sir. The discovery was not accidental. God's own hand was in it, and the translation of the records was also divine. But you see, sir, this will not be information that all of England will embrace. I know. I resisted it strenuously myself, and my wife as well. Our neighbor, Emmeline Plowhurst . . ."

"Yes, the young lady who died of pneumonia in your house. Dreadful incident. Dr. Driscoll told me. But I still don't see why that should drive you from these shores."

"Emmeline was being starved to break her faith in the book I told you of. Despite our resistance, we felt we owed it to Emmeline to at least see why she was willing to die for it. My wife started it, and quite surprised she was to discover that she could not see it as a charlatan's invention. We even quarreled over it, but she pointed out what I could not deny: She had read it and therefore could judge it; I had not. When I did, I came around to her view."

The squire's face hardened.

"Sir, I am not proselytizing. I am merely explaining. We—my wife and I and our maid, little Madge—read the work and prayed together. All of us. To a person, we felt the Lord had confirmed what none of us wanted. I still wish it were not so. Can you believe I would do this for anything less than to serve God? It's certainly no service to me personally."

The old squire continued to glare fiercely at the one he had always befriended, whose qualities he had recognized, whose abilities he had nourished and publicized. He could not misinterpret or ignore the anguish he read in Henry's answering gaze, and his expression softened. "I don't pretend to understand, hanged if I do, but I know you believe in what you're doing and I'll not cut across your right to it. But what would I do with your wheelwright business? Your farm perhaps. It's a fine bit of land, but . . ."

"My journeyman, Hector Greene, could take over my shop. He's prepared, I believe. He knows my clients. You could, perhaps, arrange to have him buy the business from you, over time, with a share of his profits. I think he would be more than pleased with such an arrangement, and I think you would not be severely damaged by it."

A twinkle or a shadow of humor somehow made it through the old man's reserve. Henry had always had the confidence of his own worth, and his proposition, if a bit cheeky, appealed to the old gentleman. "Suppose you're right, Henry. Wouldn't do me harm. Blast it, I wish you would reconsider. Stay here where you belong. There must be a better solution."

"I've a wife and children who will share in the consequences of my choice, sir. How can I guarantee their gentle acceptance among associates here?"

"I see, of course. But why do you think it will be any better in America?"

"Perhaps it won't, but we will settle where others will be who share our belief. It may be that their community can use a wheelwright."

※

Henry left Squire Farnsworth considerably relieved, first because the squire, though once again disappointed in him, still regarded him with kindness, and second, because he had agreed to purchase both his farm and his business.

Hector listened with interest when Henry explained that he could actually become the proprietor of the wheelwright shop; yet he argued heatedly with Henry's motives.

"Hector, lad, believe me, I know what I'm about. I don't have limitless wealth. I'm not gentry, like the squire. I own this quiet little corner and depend upon it to sustain me and my family. When I am judged a heretic, as I surely will be . . ."

"A wot, sir?"

"A heretic. That's a person judged by his society to have abandoned accepted religion and separated himself from their orthodox community."

"Don't understand none of that, sir."

"I didn't expect you would. Doesn't matter. When people begin to see me as a heretic, there will be no more business."

"I ain't all that religious myself, sir. Don't go to no church. Never did. Me aunt, now, she's been after me right enough." He chuckled. "Calls me a 'eathen, she does. Maybe I won't get no more business than you, sir."

"I wouldn't worry, Hector. You've learned enough to do good work, and people expect to deal with heathens. They're quite forgiving of them. Not heretics. Heathens can still be saved; heretics are by nature too depraved for anything short of crucifixion."

Hector shrugged. It was a deeper matter than he cared to plumb. All he seemed to gather was that Henry would be going to

America and he, Hector, was to become beholden to Squire Farnsworth, who would take a regular amount of his profits and apply it toward the purchase of the shop. He did not like the arrangement but trusted Henry's judgment enough to agree to it.

The first phase of Henry's plans had gone well, but thereafter scenes from his nightmares seemed tamer and more comforting. His older sisters cycled through shrill accusations, soulful pleading, frigid silence, and threats of fratricide. His two brothers-in-law, predictably, refused further sociability with him and his family, and when Henry's solicitor delivered an amount to each of them that corresponded to what Henry deemed a fair and equitable share in Horse Stone, they grumbled at his niggardly lack of largesse, apparently oblivious to the fact that the title-holder had no obligation to share holdings that were legally his alone. Temperance, genuinely grieved, thanked him tearfully, even as she pleaded with him to reconsider his decision to emigrate.

The Smirthwaite household was hardly a bulwark of solace or reprieve. The squire voiced blatant disapproval, and his wife promptly suffered nervous collapse, and when that failed to produce the expected capitulation, she seemed to recover rather quickly and find strength to renounce her wayward daughter roundly and swear never to utter another word to her or recognize her or her children ever again. Lydia saw in her eyes hurt, anger, and resentment beyond anything she had imagined. The expression bore such flinty intransigence that Lydia understood in that instant that she would never be admitted again. She was rejected, and it took all her aristocratic reserve to walk out of the house of her childhood with the dignity of her faith and the determination that she would not be coerced, certain now that she could follow Henry's lead. Nora also fell under Mrs. Smirthwaite's hot indignation and once again fled to Horse Stone's shelter.

It was as Henry had feared. His dear old nation would always claim her share of high-minded, even-handed good men, such as Squire Farnsworth, Hugh Morecroft, and Dr. Driscoll. And there were many like Hector Greene, impartial and indifferent, who would never have raised any complaint against an aberrant religion; and there were the few who had suffered severely enough to have learned tolerance, such as Howard Hamilton. But those noble, impartial, tolerant few could hardly offset the sweeping condemnation heaped upon them by the majority, who had decreed ostracism and hostility.

The sale of Horse Stone gave Henry the competence he needed for passage to America, although he had not counted on the necessity of including Nora. That would leave less revenue for obtaining land in America. There was, of course, no remedy for that. Squire Farnsworth did not insist on hasty appropriation of Horse Stone, but Henry was sure little good could come of lengthy delay. Within less than a month, they bundled their transportable goods into trunks and Hector helped them load them on the heavy wagon that now belonged to Squire Farnsworth, and they made the two-day journey to Liverpool, with an over-night rest at an inn *en route*.

The day of their departure dawned gray and misty. Spirits were low, and only the conviction of necessity and the fact that passage was already purchased could overcome the pall of the moment. Though the sun had not fully risen, in the growing light they could see that a greasy film tinctured the surface of the water, and the senses did not happily assimilate the smells of the sea, heterogeneous freight, motley crowds, a few passengers with foodstuffs for the journey, the harsh sounds of barked commands, chatter and complaints among crew and passengers. A few were jovial and quite eager for the journey ahead. Most appeared heavy-spirited and reluctant, or so it seemed to Henry and Lydia. Madge and Nora hardly spoke, and Lydia was sure they were trembling with anticipation, yet she saw Madge smile, then noticed that her attention was on one of the passengers, a man from the Mormon congregation, the one with whom Lydia had been quite curt on their first visit to the warehouse/chapel. Lydia groaned inside. They would be fellow passengers all across the ocean. She would have to find a way to make amends for her snobbery. She saw that he joined a rather numerous group of travelers, many of whom Lydia and Henry had come to know peripherally through their brief association with the Mormon congregation. They then, like the Glendrakes, were emigrating to America, with the hope of great opportunity, or perhaps like Henry and Lydia, the hope of acceptance among fellow believers. Undeniably, there was comfort in the fact that the ship would be carrying others of the same persuasion.

There was an urgent press when the call came to approach the gangplank for boarding. The young emigrant who had drawn Madge's attention and the group he had joined all began boarding together. The young man's demeanor led Lydia to assume that they all must be Mormon, because they seemed to bond immediately. She wondered if their own little party should join them, but Henry's attention was elsewhere. Far back in the morning shadows, a couple pushed themselves through the peddlers and dock workers, followed by a third figure a few paces behind. Their eagerness to reach the departing travelers' group might have identified them as late arrivals, but even in the dimness of morning twilight, Henry recognized them.

He cried out, "Hugh! Temperance!" He broke into a run toward them and they quickened their steps to meet him. The third figure approached more slowly. It was Howard Hamilton. Henry seized Hugh's hand and wrung it vigorously. Hugh responded by releasing Henry's grip and folding him in a voiceless embrace, closing his eyes tightly against the tears he could not restrain. Temperance wept openly. Lydia by now had also approached the group and Temperance circled her in her embrace, her weeping now easier with Lydia's shoulder to rest against. Howard stood silently by, his head bowed.

Henry finally spoke. "Thank you, Hugh, and you, my little sister. It's . . ."

Lydia finished his sentence. "It's comforting to know someone still . . . that there are warm feelings . . ." She sniffed noisily. "We had . . . I had almost decided no one would . . ."

Temperance extended a small package to Lydia, a box wrapped in a linen cloth. "Catherine learned of our intentions to meet you," Temperance explained, drying her eyes. "She asked me to bring you this." She paused. "She truly wanted to come with us. Her husband intervened."

Lydia, her eyes still wet, opened the package slowly. In the box was an elegant emerald bracelet. She raised her eyes again but could see only through the blur of her tears. "She . . . she remembers. Catherine remembers. She doesn't hate me."

Temperance answered softly. "No. She doesn't hate you. How could she?"

Howard stepped forward. "Wish you were staying, Henry. Hanged if I know why you have to do this."

Henry smiled the wry smile of one who understands raw irony. "Mr. Hamilton, no one knows why better than you. Emmeline surely has not left our thoughts. But thanks for missing us a little."

"Little? Not a little, Henry. You stood by Emmeline when everyone else misunderstood. We won't forget that."

Lydia hugged him. "Take care of her girls. We'll see them again, I hope," she managed.

"I hope so too, Lydia. I sincerely hope you will come back to us."

"Thank you. All of you," Henry said. "Hugh, all the way to Liverpool. Two days! Why didn't you tell us?"

"I'm afraid we hadn't planned to come at first," Hugh said. "Then I . . . I got to thinking how long the rest of mortality is. And when I met Mr. Hamilton, together we realized we could not send you off without . . . well, you had already left when we decided to be here for your send-off. We were perhaps two hours behind you." His voice broke, though he went on speaking. "Perhaps I still don't agree with your motives, but even as I say it, I know you could do no less. Perhaps I envy you."

The sun had begun to show itself, its orange rim just visible now about the horizon. Voices reached them from the deck of the ship, and a male voice, a full-throated baritone from the group they assumed were Mormons, began singing.

The morning breaks,
The shadows flee.

The singer hesitated, and it appeared to Lydia that he was urging his fellows to join him. He began again, and this time several others did indeed join in. The melody had to be a familiar one, for they all seemed to stay on key.

The morning breaks,
The shadows flee.

Other voices joined now, and a few actually sang harmony—an alto here, a bass there. There were not many, but they blended nicely. Lydia remarked to herself that it was much better than music that they had been regaled with during their first visit to Emmeilne's congregation, the day they first met Heber Kimball.

The man with the rich baritone must have had musical training. He seemed to be their leader, urging them to united harmony. The impromptu choir might have been more exquisitely tuned, a bit more precise, but the overall effect was surprisingly pleasant.

The morning breaks,
The shadows flee.
Lo, Zion's standard is unfurled.
The dawning of a brighter day
Majestic rises on the world.

Hugh, Temperance, and Howard stood quietly listening as the strains of the hymn drifted down to them.

"Astonishing!" said Hugh. "Quite lovely. Who is that group?"

"They're probably all Mormons, Hugh," Henry said a bit wryly.

"Who is the leader? Remarkable voice. Lovely baritone," Hugh added.

"I don't know him," Henry answered. "It appears that a number of those we know have friends we *don't* know. Our journey seems a bit less dreary, though, if they plan to sing to us on the way."

The three who had come to see them off managed a rueful smile, then grew solemn again.

"You must go then?" Hugh asked.

Henry nodded. "We have to follow our faith, Hugh," Henry assured. "Just as you have to live your . . . What did you call it? From Saint James, you said. Your 'royal law.' "

"Thank you for the reminder. It is my path."

A bell clanged from the ship, warning that the gangplank would be lifted soon.

"The *Brittania*," Temperance mused, wiping her eyes. "A ship of that name is what takes you away from us?"

"No ship can take Britain from us. We go because we must, but England will go with us. So will your love," Lydia said as she folded Temperance in a final embrace.

About the Author

Horse Stone House, the home of Henry and Lydia Glendrake, stands in Eccleston, Lancashire, England, the actual ancestral dwelling of Harold K. Moon's great-grandfather, Henry Moon, converted to Mormonism by Heber C. Kimball in 1838.

Moon has not been violent with history, but is not so gentle that he hesitated when strict historical accuracy could not accommodate itself to the flow of his narrative. He has been faithful to his ancestors' spiritual stamina.

Born in Mesa, Arizona, Moon has lived in varied circumstances and far-flung places. The happy husband of Mayva Magleby and the father of nine noble and productive children, he now enjoys the fictitious leisure of retirement in Orem, Utah.